CW00739590

Fruit Cake and Fear

A
Péridale Café
MYSTERY

AGATHA FROST

For questions and comments about this book, please contact
pinktreepublishing@gmail.com

www.pinktreepublishing.com
www.agathafrost.com

Edited by Keri Lierman and Karen Sellers
Proofread by Eve Curwen

ISBN: 9781549627989
Imprint: Independently published

A Peridale Cafe MYSTERY

Book Eight

CHAPTER 1

"**H**appy Birthday, Julia!" Evelyn exclaimed as she handed over a lilac envelope. "I made it myself. I hope you like it."

Julia paused making a pot of tea to accept the card with a grateful smile. She looked at Evelyn's handwriting, which was as eccentric and unique as her personality. This was the sixth card Julia had received so far from her customers, but Evelyn's was the first that had been handmade.

"That's so kind of you." Julia ripped open the envelope. "I hope you didn't go to too much trouble."

Julia slid the textured card out of the envelope, looking down at its bizarre design with an unsure smile. Instead of the usual message of '*Happy Birthday!*', Evelyn had opted for a system of random lilac dots, which were connected by glittering gold lines.

"It's your astrological birth chart," Evelyn said eagerly as she leaned over and peered at the intricate design. "Each dot shows the position of the planets during their orbit of the sun at the *exact* time and date of your birth. It's the key to unlocking your personality!"

"It's beautiful," Julia said, her heart swelling. "This is so thoughtful."

"It's creepy," Dot, Julia's gran, mumbled from the table nearest the counter, pausing before sipping her tea. "How did you know the *exact* time and date of Julia's birth, Evelyn? Been digging through her bins?"

"*All* birth records are public," Evelyn said as she shifted her blue turban, which had a matching brooch in the centre. "I'm also wearing your birthstone colour, sapphire, to celebrate your special day. Sapphire was once thought to guard against evil and poisoning."

"Planning on getting poisoned today, Julia?" Dot called over Evelyn's shoulder.

Julia shot her gran a look that she hoped read '*behave*', but she knew it would be in vain. Dot was a fierce woman who had a razor-sharp tongue and a lightning-quick mind, even if she did have a heart of gold underneath it. When it came to Evelyn's eccentric ways, her patience was as thin as it got.

"It was traditionally a favourite stone of priests and kings," Evelyn continued, undeterred by Dot's comments. "It also symbolises purity and wisdom, and you're the purest woman I know."

"I wish it was my birthday every day," Julia said with a chuckle as she opened the card to read Evelyn's sweet message. "You're too kind. I'll treasure this."

"I've loaded this with the energy of the universe," Evelyn said, reaching into her silk kaftan to pull out a sapphire crystal. "You're never more powerful than on the day of your birth, but it's also when you're most susceptible to the negative frequencies in the ether. Make sure to keep safe, and maybe get home early today. I sense a terrible storm is coming, and I'd hate for you to get stuck in the café on your birthday."

"Or maybe she heard the weather report this morning?" Dot mumbled through pursed lips as she pushed up her curls. "What a load of *codswallop!*"

"I must go," Evelyn said, glancing over her shoulder at Dot with a strained smile. "I have guests checking into the B&B in an hour, and I still haven't burned sage in the rooms to cleanse the energies of the last guests. You know how it is."

Evelyn bowed before swishing around, the silk of her kaftan floating behind her as she headed to the door, one eye trained on Dot as she left.

"Why can't she predict *useful* things?" Dot sighed as she topped up her teacup before dropping in two cubes of sugar. "I'd love for her to guess my lottery numbers, or the day I'm going to die."

"You want to know when you're going to die?" Jessie, Julia's young lodger and café apprentice, said as she came out of the kitchen with a fresh batch of red velvet cupcakes. "That's grim."

"I want to make sure I'm wearing my *best* clothes," Dot said casually as she adjusted the brooch holding her stiff blouse collar in place. "Who wants to get hit by a bus wearing socks with holes in them?"

Fruit Cake and Fear

Julia chuckled as she looked over Evelyn's card again. She looked down at the arrangement of the planets as they would have been thirty-eight years ago, and she thought about her mother giving birth to her under those planets. She was not sure she believed in energies and spirits like Evelyn, but Julia never felt more connected to her mother than on her birthday.

"Well, I have this crystal from Evelyn, so I shouldn't get hit by any buses today," Julia said as she clutched the jagged piece of blue glass. "I wonder if she's right about that storm."

"They said something about it on the television this morning," Dot said. "Some nonsense about a serious weather warning, but when are they ever right about those things? If I constantly wore my raincoat every time they predicted rain, I'd be sleeping in the thing! They're about as useful at predicting the weather as Evelyn is the future!"

"She might be right," Jessie said as she peered out of the café window. "It's getting quite dark out there."

Julia glanced at the clock. It was not even lunchtime, but Jessie was right about it being unusually dark for the time of day.

"I must dash, love," Dot said after draining her

cup. "I'll see you tonight for your birthday dinner."

Dot shuffled out of the café with a wave of her hand and hurried across the village green towards her small cottage. Before she slipped through her front door, she looked up at the darkening sky and shook her head.

"It's all people are posting about online," Jessie said as she scrolled through her phone. "They're saying it's the worst storm the Cotswolds has seen in twenty years."

"And on my birthday too," Julia mumbled, glancing at the clock again. "Let's hold out for now. It might just pass right over us."

Jessie looked up at the sky again as the clouds gathered, before shrugging, and stuffing her phone back into the pocket of her baggy jeans. She grabbed one of the cupcakes from the tray on the counter and crammed it into her mouth.

The bell above the door rang out, and Julia's oldest friend, Roxy Carter, hurried into the café, followed by a gust of wind that ripped the door out of her hand, slamming it in its frame.

"It's blowing a gale out there!" Roxy cried as she flattened down her flame red hair. "It's all the teachers have been talking about since this morning's meeting. We're sending the kids home early to be safe, and we haven't done that since the bad snow two years ago."

"Maybe one of Evelyn's predictions will come true for once," Jessie said with a smirk as she began to sweep the already clean café floor. "I suspect we'll see pigs flying past the window in the next ten minutes."

Roxy laughed as she unzipped the large handbag on her shoulder. She reached inside and pulled out a white envelope and a book.

"I had no idea what to get you for your birthday, so I've put a voucher in the card." Roxy handed over the envelope with an apologetic smile. "But, I *did* find this. I thought it might put a smile on your face."

Roxy placed the book on the counter, and Julia recognised it in an instant.

"Our yearbook!" Julia exclaimed as she looked down at the '*Hollins High School Class of 1995*' front cover. "Where did you find this?"

"Mum was going through some things in the attic. She's got it in her head that she wants to put her spare bedrooms on *Airbnb* now that she's alone in that big house, even though she hates people touching her things. Can you believe our school was doing yearbooks before it was the '*cool*' thing? I swear the only reason we did it was because of that American exchange program some of the teachers went on when we were in Year Seven."

"I think that's the only reason they called our end of year disco '*the prom*'," Julia said with a chuckle as she picked up the book. "It didn't take away from the fact it was in the school gym with the world's cheapest buffet and a CD player instead of a DJ."

Julia flicked through the pages, her high school memories flooding back. She had been on the yearbook team with Roxy, and it had been their job to gather all of the photographs and stories from their classmates and teachers, and assemble them in the book. Their school's ancient computers had not been capable of putting together a yearbook, so they had done everything by hand, before photocopying the pages, laminating them, and binding them with a spiral.

Julia flicked through the dog-eared plastic pages, landing on a grainy picture of a school trip to London they had taken in Year Ten. Teenage versions of Julia and Roxy grinned up from the mists of time in front of Buckingham Palace, along with some other girls from their year with whom they had since lost contact.

Fruit Cake and Fear

"It makes me feel relatively ancient," Roxy said with a sigh as she assessed her reflection in a small compact mirror. "When did we get so old?"

"Speak for yourself," Julia said, tossing her curls over her shoulder. "I like to think I'm getting better with age."

"Like a fine wine?" Roxy suggested.

"Or cheese," Jessie added.

"Cheese gets mouldy eventually," Roxy said as she snapped the mirror shut. "I was lying in bed with Violet last week, and she said the lines around my eyes looked cute. *Cute!* I never even knew I had them. You're lucky Barker isn't younger than you because I feel myself hurtling towards forty at lightning speed and it's terrifying me."

"Well, my life has never been better," Julia said, smiling at Jessie over Roxy's shoulder as she took the mirror from her friend. She lifted it up to her makeup-free face and creased up her eyes. "Although you're right about the lines."

"Violet said they were *experience* lines," Roxy scoffed as she took back the mirror and dropped it in her handbag. "I'll see if she's saying that when she gets to our age. Do you remember those awards that we all had to vote for?" Roxy flicked to the back pages of the book. "I got *Most Likely To Be Famous* because I was convinced I was going to be discovered and asked to be a pop star. Another couple of years and I totally would have been asked to be in the Spice Girls."

"You really *are* old," Jessie mumbled as she shuffled past with the brush. "They're so retro."

"*Retro?*" Roxy cried, her cheeks flushing. "You kids could learn a bit about *Girl Power!* Has it really been that long?"

"Well, we left school twenty-two years ago," Julia said as she found her own award. "And I got *Most Likely To Be A Baker.* Took me long enough, but I got there eventually."

"Feels like twenty-two minutes sometimes," Roxy said wistfully as she stared into the corner of the room. "Treasure your life, Jessie. It will whizz by in the blink of an eye."

Jessie looked down her nose at Roxy before shrugging and carrying on with the sweeping. Julia turned to the next page, which contained surly portraits of all their teachers. It had been so long, Julia had almost forgotten most of their names. As she scanned the vaguely familiar faces, she suddenly realised she was now a similar age to most of them.

"Can I keep this for a couple of days?" Julia carefully closed the book of memories and held it to her chest. "I haven't seen mine since I moved back from London."

"Keep it," Roxy said, holding her hands up as she dragged her handbag back over her shoulder. "My mum has a whole box of them. I got lumbered with the ones nobody wanted to buy, which was quite a lot. It will give you something to read tonight when the storm hits."

"I hope we don't flood like last time." Julia peered through the window as increasingly darker clouds drifted in from a distance. "Gran had sandbags piled up to the top of her door and had Amy Clark hand her food through the window because she refused to come out until it stopped raining."

"Dot *is* insane," Jessie said as she swept past them again. "*Actually* insane."

"I should get going," Roxy said as she glanced back at the window. "Since I'm finishing work early, I thought I'd buy some ice cream and wine, and have a movie night with Violet."

"*Pretty Woman?*" Julia asked.

"You already know that's the first thing we're watching," Roxy replied with a wink. "I think Violet hates the fact that she now knows the film word for word, and she'd never even seen it before she met me."

"I sympathise with Violet," Jessie mumbled.

"We used to watch that film every weekend when we'd have sleepovers at your house," Julia said, the memory warming her. "Remember that time we were quoting the lines along with the film, and your sister, Rachel, filmed us and showed it to that boy you had a crush on?"

"He never spoke to me again," Roxy said, pinching between her eyes as she laughed softly. "Maybe that was for the best."

"Let me make you a latte for the road," Julia said, already grabbing a cardboard cup from under the counter. "I think it might be the last coffee I make today if the clouds keep rolling in."

Julia quickly made Roxy her usual latte and bagged up a chocolate brownie for her on the house. When she left, Julia leaned against the counter and flicked through the memories as the sky outside continued to darken.

"I never had a yearbook," Jessie said as she turned her head upside down to look at the pictures. "Never even finished school."

"It's all a bit silly," Julia said when she noticed the tinge of sadness in Jessie's voice. "Look at this. This girl here wrote '*I will miss you so much, Julia!*', and I haven't spoken to her in more than twenty years."

"It's still memories."

"You're making memories right now," Julia reminded her. "Sweeping this floor before the storm will be a memory. Besides, you're at college with Dolly and Dom. I didn't make any friends when I was at college. They all called me the teacher's pet because I always finished first. They hated me."

"The curse of being the best baker in Peridale," Jessie said with a wink as she continued to sweep. "My heart *bleeds* for you."

Julia chuckled as she slapped the old book shut. She peered through the window and watched as parents collected their kids from St. Peter's Primary School. Cars sped away, while some parents ran across the village green with their little ones close by their side, umbrellas already primed for the downpour.

"Maybe I should cancel my birthday dinner?" Julia thought aloud as she drummed her fingers on the counter. "I don't want people driving up that winding lane to my cottage in the rain."

"But you've spent all morning baking that cake," Jessie called from the kitchen as she emptied the contents of the dustpan into the bin. "The fruit cake that you said was full of fruit but isn't technically fruitcake."

"It's a fruit cake for people who don't like fruitcake," Julia called back. "One of my mother's old recipes. It's a cinnamon sponge with pieces of crystallised dried fruit, spiced apple cream in between the slices, with hidden strawberry jam in the middle. Top it off with chocolate cream and cinnamon powdered raspberries and blueberries, and you've got something that's hard to hate."

"Exactly," Jessie said as she popped her head through the beaded curtain. "You can't let it go to – "

Before Jessie could finish her sentence, a deep rumble of thunder cut her off. It boomed through the village, echoing around the small café.

"Please tell me that was your stomach?" Julia asked hopefully.

A second rumble of thunder moaned above the café. They looked up at the ceiling as sudden rain beat down on the slate roof.

"*Cool.*" Jessie exclaimed with a wicked grin. "It's bouncing off the road!"

They hurried over to the window as the sky turned a deep shade of purple, only illuminating when a crack of lightning ripped through the clouds, followed by another ominous growl of thunder. Through the golf-ball sized raindrops, Julia was sure she saw her gran's curtains whipping shut.

It only took a matter of seconds for the village green to clear of people, and for Julia to realise that her café would be completely empty for the rest of the day.

"Maybe we should close early," Jessie suggested as the air began to thicken. "Just this once."

"It *is* my birthday."

"Exactly."

"People will understand."

"They'll think you're *bonkers* if you don't."

They looked at each other with devious smiles as they glanced back at the kitchen where their coats were hanging. Julia could not remember the last time she had closed her café due to the weather conditions, but she could also not remember the last time she had seen the road in front of her café turn into a river in a matter of minutes.

They headed into the kitchen without another word. Julia locked the back door while Jessie made sure all the equipment was turned off. Even though fewer than a couple of minutes had passed since the rain had started, it beat down heavier with each new drop.

"I'll write a note," Julia said before pulling the pen lid off with her teeth. "Just in case the storm passes."

She quickly scribbled down '*Closed due to adverse weather – Sorry for the inconvenience*', and stuck it to the glass panel in the door with a piece of tape. The condensation dampened the paper and made the blue ink bleed, but it was still legible.

Jessie took off her apron and pulled her black hood low over her face. Julia pulled on her pink pea coat, which was missing a hood, but her car was only parked in the alley between her café and the post office. They flicked off the lights, casting the café into such darkness, Julia would have sworn summer was over, and Mother Nature had skipped autumn and gone straight to winter, despite it only being the middle of September.

"I've got my crystal," Julia said, clutching Evelyn's sapphire in her palm. "She said it would ward off evil."

"Did she mention anything about rain?" Jessie replied as she wrapped her hand around the door handle. "Ready?"

"No."

"*Tough.*"

Jessie pulled open the door, and it became

Fruit Cake and Fear

obvious neither of them were prepared for what was waiting for them. The door flew out of her hand and hit the wall behind it, the glass rattling, and the piece of paper fluttering. The wind poured into the café, bringing the heavy rain with it. A puddle formed around Julia's feet in seconds, but it was too late to turn back.

Julia thrust her car keys into Jessie's hand and pushed her out into the rain. Her young apprentice stumbled backwards for a second, the wind threatening to blow her away, before ducking into the alley. Holding her breath, Julia stepped out and closed the door.

Despite the stuffy air, the rain was freezing and soaked her through in seconds. She stabbed the brass key at the lock, desperate to find the hole. She battled to keep her eyes open, but the rain was so heavy, it stuck her curls to her face. She swept her wet locks out of her eyes and squinted through the water, relieved when the key slotted into where it should.

After locking the door, she ran around the side of the café. The wind battering against her almost knocked her clean off her feet, but she fought back; even though it was a completely flat surface, she felt as if she was trying to climb the steepest hill.

She slipped down the alley and to the driver's side of her vintage aqua blue Ford Anglia, but Jessie was the one sitting behind the wheel when she opened the door.

"Not a chance!" Julia cried over another rumble of thunder. "*Move!*"

"But I'm retaking my test soon," Jessie protested, her fingers tightening around the wheel. "Barker said I need the practice."

"I doubt Barker wanted you to practice during a monsoon!" Julia cried, her teeth chattering. "I'm soaked to the bone!"

Jessie sighed and rolled her eyes before yanking off her belt and climbing over the gearstick to the passenger seat. She slumped down and glared at Julia from under her hood.

"I didn't want to drive your crap car anyway," Jessie mumbled as she wiped her damp hair out of her face. "It's probably going to wash away and kill us before we get to the cottage."

"Thanks for the vote of confidence." Julia yanked the belt across her chest. "She might be vintage, but the old girl has got me through a lot. Besides, I have Evelyn's crystal, don't I?"

They both shared a little smirk before Julia bravely slotted the key into the ignition and reversed the car down to the opening of the alley. She rested her arm on the back of Jessie's seat as she attempted to look through the back window, but all she could see was the cascading water.

Julia flicked on her headlights, which illuminated the falling rain ahead. She could barely see more than a couple of metres in front of the car, but she could see her cottage in her mind's eye, and she was confident she could get there. She pulled the sapphire out of her pocket and placed it on the dashboard.

Tightening her fingers around the steering wheel, Julia crawled forward, her eyes focussed on the little she could see of the road ahead. She gasped as a bolt of lightning fractured the black sky, illuminating the village for a brief moment. A rumble of thunder followed almost immediately; Julia felt it in her bones. Jessie looked at her with a wide grin, but Julia did not share her companion's enthusiasm. She tried to look back at her café in the rear-view mirror, but the rain had already swallowed it up.

"*Look out!*" Jessie cried.

Julia instinctively slammed her foot on the brakes before her eyes re-joined the narrow beams of light ahead. A man in a floor-length black trench coat had appeared inches in front of her car. Julia's heart pounded in her chest as she stared at the man she had almost hit, and it only intensified when the stranger looked up from under his hood, the headlights illuminating his face.

"*Barker*?" Julia mumbled, a mixture of relief and dread circling in her chest.

Barker hurried around the car and jumped into the backseat as another bolt of lightning and thunder happened simultaneously.

"Nice weather we're having," Barker said through chattering teeth as he yanked down his hood. "I should have known it was the wrong time to grab lunch, but the thought of your chocolate cake was too tempting to resist."

"I could have hit you." Julia glanced back at him through the mirror. "Why were you walking on the road?"

"I saw your headlights and figured it must be you. I wanted to attract your attention."

"It's a good job *some* of us are looking out for hazards," Jessie said firmly. "I'm going to ace my test with my eyes closed."

Julia continued to crawl forward and rounded the village green before driving to the opening of the lane that led to her cottage. As the road steepened, her car struggled against the flowing stream. With the extra weight in the back seat, she changed down a gear and pushed her foot hard onto the accelerator.

Even though she knew the lane's twists and turns by memory, she drove as slowly as she dared. Lightning cracked periodically above them, illuminating the road ahead for a brief moment before darkness descended again, bringing the thunder with it.

"We must be in the middle of this thing," Barker mumbled as he peered out of the window. "I read that something was coming, but I didn't expect it to be this –"

Barker's voice trailed off as bright headlights raced towards Julia's car, blinding her in an instant. She swerved out of the way, but the lane was narrow. She felt the front of her car crunch into the low stone wall as a car sped past them, rocking her tiny vintage car.

"What a *moron*!" Jessie cried, twisting in her seat to watch as the headlights vanished. "If it wasn't raining I'd get out and chase the idiot!"

Julia stared ahead at the lights as they hit the wall and bounced back at her. She twisted her key in the ignition, the engine coughing and spluttering back at her.

"At least things can't get any worse," Barker said with an awkward laugh.

As though to mock him, the heavens opened to send down the biggest crack of lightning Julia had ever seen. The thunder shook the road beneath as the purple streaks leaked across the dark sky. They soon faded away but were replaced just as quickly with fresh bolts. A slither of lightening fractured away from the network of neon lights, cracking against a wooden telegraph pole metres from Julia's car. The power lines sparked and fizzed, snapping away from the wooden pole as it began to fall. Julia held her breath and turned her engine over again, but it was in vain; her car was dead.

Like a tree falling in the wilderness, they watched as the heavy pole drifted through the rain, its descent illuminated by more lightning. Julia let out a small sigh of relief when the pole began to fall away from her car, but it was short-lived when she realised exactly where they were on the winding lane.

Julia closed her eyes and listened to the almighty crunch of stone and wood as the pole found its target. When she opened them, another show of lightning treated her to the mess ahead. Even through the heavy rain, she could see the damage the fallen pole had caused.

Fruit Cake and Fear

"My cottage," Barker mumbled as the thunder swallowed them up. "It's *destroyed* my cottage."

CHAPTER 2

The sun shone brightly the next morning, but it felt like dark clouds were still circling Barker's cottage. Julia hung back with him on the other side of the garden wall as the large crane attached to the fire engine lifted the pole from where his sitting room used to be. She supportively looped her fingers around his as more of the thatched roof crumbled away.

Fruit Cake and Fear

"I wouldn't go in there if I were you," the lead firefighter said as he walked away from the cottage, pulling off his yellow hat. "Best thing to do now is to start documenting what happened from out here for the insurance people."

Barker nodded, his hand tightening around Julia's. They watched as the crane lifted the pole over the side of the wall and onto the road. They unclipped it, retracted the crane, and headed off down the winding lane, leaving the charred chunk of wood on the side of the narrow lane. Despite their advice, Barker pulled his keys from his pocket and unclipped the garden gate.

Julia followed him to the front door, her eyes trained on the giant hole in the front of his cottage. A mess of bricks and glass covered all of his ultra-modern furniture; it was barely recognisable.

The part of the cottage that was still standing creaked as Barker unlocked the door. He swung it open in its frame and peered down the hallway before stepping inside. Julia followed him in, her shoes squelching against the soaked carpet. She looked up through a hole in the roof, the cloudless sky mocking them from above.

Barker forced open the door to the sitting room, and Julia's hand immediately drifted up to her mouth. The entire front wall and half of the roof were completely missing. They climbed over the splayed rubble and stared through the large hole at the bright blue sky. Somehow, it looked even worse from the inside.

"Your dining room is okay," Julia said as she walked through the intact arch to the next room. "There's a little water damage, but it's still standing."

She traced her finger along the wet glass table, her eyes landing on the typewriter in the corner. The sheet of paper that Barker had been working on had been completely saturated and now hugged the keys of the ancient machine. Barker followed her in and picked up an equally soaked stack of papers.

"The whole book," he cried. "It's *ruined*."

"Didn't you make copies?" Julia asked as she peeked into the kitchen, which looked entirely untouched.

"No," he said, tossing the stack onto the table with a splatter. "Nor do I have home insurance. It was on the to-do list when I first moved in, but I kept putting it off. Everything is ruined."

Julia peeled back the top page of the crime novel Barker had been working on. The sheet tore down the middle under her touch, the ink bleeding together even more.

Fruit Cake and Fear

"It's just stuff," Julia said hopefully as a pigeon flew through the hole and planted itself on the pile of rubble. "You can start the book again."

"And the giant hole in my cottage?"

"I'm sure it's not as bad as it looks," Julia mumbled, the wobble in her voice letting her know she did not believe that any more than Barker did. "You can stay with me while we figure it out."

"I don't want to impose."

"It's only temporary," she said reassuringly as she walked around the dining room table. "I already spoke about it with Jessie last night, and she agreed. You're there half of the week anyway. What other choice do you have?"

"I could stay at Evelyn's B&B," Barker said, giving her the first smile she had seen from him all morning. "A free tarot reading with breakfast might be fun. If only she had foreseen this and warned me. It would have reminded me to buy some damn insurance."

Julia pulled the sapphire crystal from her pocket and turned it over in her fingers. Between crashing her beloved car and witnessing the destruction of Barker's cottage, she was beginning to wonder if Evelyn had cursed the birthstone.

Julia followed Barker into his bedroom, which

was in perfect condition. Two large bikes, one with a pink bow wrapped around the handlebars, rested against his wardrobe.

"Your birthday present," Barker said, pinching between his eyes as he sucked the air through his teeth. "I forgot all about them with everything that's happened. I thought it would be nice to ride them out into the country together on Sundays and have picnics."

"It's almost like you knew I was going to crash my car." Julia tiptoed up to Barker and kissed him on the cheek. "I love it."

Barker wrapped his arms around Julia and pulled her into a tight hug. For the first time since she had met him, she could sense that he was scared, and it unsettled her. She could not begin to imagine how she would have felt if the telegraph pole had fallen through her cottage.

After bagging up as many clothes as he could carry, Barker set off up the lane to his new temporary home with his typewriter wedged under his arm. Julia waited until he was out of view before she wheeled her new bike out of the destroyed cottage. When she was on the road, she unravelled the pink bow and looked down at her birthday present. The last time she had ridden a bike was as a little girl, but hers had not been as pretty as this one. Its twisted metal structure was a similar shade of blue as her car. The wheels were soft cream. The handlebars and seat were covered in camel coloured leather with cream stitching, and there was a little metal basket at the front, which was lined with floral printed fabric. She had never expected such a gift from Barker, but she was pleasantly surprised he had picked a bike that seemed to match her tastes down to the smallest detail.

Glad she had opted for jeans and a wool jumper instead of one of her usual dresses, Julia mounted the bike and headed slowly down the lane towards the heart of Peridale. The warm air licked at her hair; it was nothing like the gale that had battered her cottage throughout the night. It was almost easy to forget how bad the weather had been the day before, but when she exited the lane and reached the village green, it became obvious Barker's cottage was not the only one to have been affected by the storm.

As she weaved in and out of the fallen slate tiles from the shops' roofs, she waved to Malcolm Johnson, the leader of the Peridale Green Fingers, as members of the club attempted to clean up the scattered litter and destroyed plants on the green.

Julia reached her café and was relieved to see it

was still standing. She rode down the alley between the café and the post office, the firm wheels bouncing against the wet cobbles. She dismounted the bike and walked towards the back of the café, her relief disappearing when she saw a fallen tree draped across the lane, its trunk having smashed through the wall surrounding the yard behind her business. She opened the back gate and pushed her bike inside, the leaves of the tree casting a shadow across the back of the café. Sighing heavily to herself, Julia beat her fist down on the metal door.

Jessie yanked on the heavy door, her brows arching when she saw Julia with the bike.

"Birthday present from Barker," Julia explained. "Have you seen this?"

Jessie stepped out of the café, her jaw dropping wide when she saw the giant tree resting against the wall, which had dispersed most of its bricks across the tiny yard.

"That's not all," Jessie said as she looked up at the leaves. "The power is out. I've been trying to steam milk and boil water on the gas, but it's taking ages."

Julia rested her bike against the wall before pulling out her phone. She dialled '*999*' and asked for the fire service. After explaining that she needed a fallen tree moved, she hung up and told Jessie to close the empty café.

With the front door locked, they set to work clearing the grey bricks out of the yard before the fire engine arrived, which the operator had explained might take a while because of the damage across the village.

"The fallen bricks have broken the slabs," Jessie said as she crouched down to run her fingers across a definite crack in one of the stones. "They're all loose."

"Those have always been a little loose," Julia said as she heaved a heavy chunk of brick out to the lane. "I've been meaning to have them fixed."

Jessie dragged the broken stone out of place, and it came away surprisingly easily. Julia was about to tell her to leave it where it was, but something underneath the stone caught her attention.

"Is that wood?" Jessie mumbled as she flipped the slab over. "How is that wood?"

Julia crouched down and ran her fingers along what looked like a wooden floorboard. They shared a confused look for a moment before Jessie pulled out the rest of the slab, which came out even easier than the first.

It exposed what appeared to be a brass hinge

connecting the wood to the concrete ground that lay behind the paved yard. Julia abandoned clearing away the rest of the fallen stone bricks and helped Jessie remove all of the heavy slabs. It became obvious very quickly that the wood formed a large door.

"I never knew your café had a basement," Jessie said as she wiped the sweat from her forehead after removing the last slab.

"Neither did I." Julia crouched and ran her fingers along a rusty padlock. "This explains why the slabs always felt loose."

Jessie moved Julia's fingers out of the way and smashed a broken piece of stone against the padlock. It popped open with a satisfying click, the tension in the wood suddenly relaxing a little.

"I *was* going to suggest we check the building plans first," Julia said as she stood up. "There might be a reason it was sealed up."

Jessie shrugged before heaving back the heavy wood door. She rested it against the café wall and stepped back to inspect her handiwork. Julia immediately clamped her hand over her nose and mouth as stale and musty air drifted up from the dark hole.

"Bloody hell," Jessie mumbled through her

sleeve. "Smells like something died down there."

Julia pulled her phone from her pocket and turned on the flashlight. She shone it down into the hole and illuminated a set of stone steps.

"Maybe we shouldn't," Julia said. "It might not be safe."

"Wimp," Jessie said, snatching the light from Julia's hand. "It might be full of pirate treasure."

Jessie hurried down the stone steps, ducking under the café and disappearing into the dark. Julia looked back at the fallen tree before sighing and following her young apprentice into the unknown.

The air was so thick and stale that Julia pulled her wool jumper over her mouth to breath. She hurried through the dark to Jessie, who was standing at the edge of the room looking down at something on a table.

"It looks like a workshop," Jessie said as she shone the light over dust covered tools and chunks of old wood. "Must have been locked up for years."

"It was a toy shop when I was a kid," Julia remembered aloud as she looked around the basement, which stretched out the length of her café and kitchen. "I could have used this as storage."

Jessie walked across the room and shone the light across a wall of shelves filled with hand-carved wooden children's toys. She paused the light on a dust-covered clown, its white face and red lips smiling eerily out at them.

"This place is *so* cool," Jessie mumbled through a grin as she moved along the rows of toys. "I can't believe we've been working above it all of this time."

"Neither can I," Julia said, glancing back at the slither of light through the opening. "Maybe we should get out of here. There might be rats, or worse."

Jessie walked away from the shelves and shone the light around the vast space. She paused on something in the corner and walked slowly across the room.

"Julia," Jessie said, her voice shaking. "I think I've found worse."

Julia joined Jessie and followed the white beam of light to the corner of the room. She grabbed Jessie at once and turned her away, holding her head against her chest.

"Is it real?" Jessie mumbled through Julia's jumper.

Julia took the light from Jessie's hand and shone it into the corner where a skeleton was propped up against the wall. The hollow eyes of the skull stared back at her, the bone completely clean. A metal

Fruit Cake and Fear

'*Head Girl*' badge glittered from the mess of rotten green and black fabric draped across the old bones, turning Julia's throat to sand.

"It's real," Julia croaked, moving the light before turning away. "And I think I know who it is."

CHAPTER 3

"Here it is." Dot pulled a newspaper clipping from the shoebox she had been rummaging through for the past five minutes. "Astrid Wood. Sixteen-years-old. Has been missing since the 29th of July, 1997."

Julia looked across Dot's dining room table and met the eyes of her old school friends, Roxy Carter and Johnny Watson. None of them needed an old clipping to remember the disappearance of Astrid Wood.

"Has it really been *that* long?" Roxy asked as she reached across the table to accept the article. "Twenty *whole* years?"

"I haven't thought about Astrid in so long," Johnny said after he accepted the clipping from Roxy. "I wrote a couple of articles about it in my early days at *The Peridale Post*, but there hasn't been any interest in ages. How do you still have this?"

"I cut out the important things from the papers and keep them," Dot said with a shrug as she flicked through the pile of clippings in the old shoebox. "Most of the recent ones involve murder cases Julia has solved. Want to see?"

"No thanks, Gran," Julia said quickly after a sip of peppermint and liquorice tea. "I think we can all remember the things that have happened in this village recently."

Johnny passed the article across the table after skimming over it. Julia accepted it, a lump growing in her throat when she looked down at the faded picture of the pretty, pale girl with the black hair. Just like in the basement, her Head Girl badge glittered from her blazer.

"She went missing the night of her Year Eleven

prom," Roxy said as she stared down into her coffee. "She was supposed to be going with Aiden Black, but she just never showed up. People thought she'd got cold feet and decided not to go, but she was never seen again."

"Until today," Jessie said as she picked furiously at the skin next to her fingernails. "She was just bones."

Dot reached across the table and squeezed Jessie's hand reassuringly, but the young girl appeared to be in a world of her own.

"Wasn't Aiden the Head Boy too?" Johnny asked as he scratched at his dark curly hair. "I know they were two years below us at school, but I'm sure they were a couple even when we were still there."

"Everyone accused him of killing her," Roxy added. "He was never charged, but people talked."

"Isn't he the one married to Doctor Black?" Dot asked as she continued to root through her box. "She's the only doctor at the surgery who doesn't talk to me like I'm a simpleton. I like her."

"Grace Black," Roxy said with a nod. "Although she was Grace Gambaccini back then."

"They live in a nice cottage over in Burford with their kids," Johnny said, his eyes glazing over as he fiddled with his thick-rimmed glasses. "I think they have three kids. I wonder how he's going to take the news. It's been so long, but I doubt he ever forgot her. I remember seeing them so in love in the canteen. I used to be so jealous."

Johnny looked awkwardly at Julia for a moment before blushing and looking down at his drink. Even back then she had known Johnny had had a crush on her, but she never saw him as anything other than a friend, something that was confirmed when they had gone on a coffee date over two years ago when Julia first returned to Peridale after twelve years away. Roxy would swear Johnny was in love with Julia to this day, but Julia did not like to think that about her friend.

Silence fell on Dot's dining room as they all stared blankly into the centre of the table. Guilt consumed Julia; she had not thought about Astrid in years. Just like everyone else in the village, she had been part of the searches in the immediate days after her disappearance. She had trawled through the countryside with Johnny and Roxy, calling out Astrid's name. The days turned to weeks, and the weeks to months, but the searches became less frequent until they stopped entirely.

"What was she like?" Jessie asked, staring blankly at her fingers as she continued to pick at the skin next to her nails.

"She was clever," Roxy said after sucking the air through her teeth. "Top of her class in most things."

"She was nice too," Johnny added. "She wasn't very popular, but she was nice. I think people used to bully her because of who her mother was."

"Are you surprised?" Roxy cried. "I wonder who's going to tell Evelyn they've found her."

"Wacky Evelyn from the B&B?" Jessie exclaimed, frowning around the table. "She had a daughter? Nobody ever mentioned it."

"The village moved on," Dot said, almost defensively. "It's been two decades. People used to ask how she was, but she'd just babble incoherently about spirits and energies. Nobody could get through to her. She dealt with it so strangely. Nobody knew what to say without setting her off, so we just left her to it."

"Poor Evelyn," Julia whispered as she looked down at the sapphire crystal in her palm. "We don't know for certain that it was Astrid yet."

"But it is," Dot said firmly as she pulled another clipping out of the box. "You said yourself she was wearing the Head Girl badge. This clipping is from the first-year anniversary of Astrid's disappearance. Evelyn pleaded in the the press for information, but nothing came of it. I don't think they bothered with her again after that."

Dot passed the clipping around the room. When it eventually reached Julia, she looked down at the considerably younger Evelyn, barely recognising the woman she had come to know as the eccentric B&B owner. Her hair was black instead of grey, and it hung freely down her face without a turban, only stopping when it reached her waist. Instead of a kaftan, she was wearing a brown poncho with flared jeans, and a dozen different coloured crystals on strings around her neck. She was clinging to a large photo of her daughter as she looked down the camera with pleading eyes. The headline read '*ONE YEAR ON – SCHOOL GIRL STILL MISSING*'. Unable to stare at Evelyn's pain anymore, Julia passed it back.

"Don't you think Astrid looks like Jessie?" Dot remarked out of the blue, breaking the sombre silence. "Quite a lot, actually."

Dot held the clipping up to Jessie's face. Julia opened her mouth to tell her gran not to be so insensitive, but when she saw the picture next to her lodger's face, the resemblance was so striking it silenced her.

"They have the same hair," Roxy said with a

nod.

"And the same dark eyes," Johnny added.

Jessie squirmed in her seat as she frowned around the table. She snatched the clipping from Dot and looked down at Astrid's school portrait.

"Looks nothing like me," Jessie mumbled as she cast the paper aside. "What happens to the café now, Julia?"

"The cold case team is crawling all over it looking for an explanation." Julia leaned back in her chair and rubbed between her eyes. "We might be closed for a while. I can't believe she was down there all that time. It feels so wrong."

"You couldn't have known," Johnny said with a sympathetic shrug. "The real question is how did she get down there?"

"Murder, of course!" Dot exclaimed, bolting up in her chair. "It has got to be."

"We don't know that, Gran."

"Yes, we do!" she insisted through pursed lips. "Who goes to the trouble of padlocking and hiding a trap door if they want it to be found? It's not like the stones put themselves there."

They all knew she was right, but it seemed none of them wanted to admit it, including Julia. It was one thing to have a teenage girl under her café for all of those years, but it was another thing entirely to know that girl had been murdered.

"Didn't you buy the shop from Alistair Black, Julia?" Dot asked as she adjusted the brooch holding her stiff collar in place. "He used to have it as a toy shop donkey's years ago."

"That explains the workshop," Jessie mumbled.

"I did, Gran," Julia said with a nod. "Although he hadn't run the shop for years when I bought it. He used to rent it out, but he wanted to get rid of it. He said it was because he didn't want to burden people with it when he died. The only reason I could afford to start again was because he gave me a good price for a quick sale."

"Alistair Black?" Johnny said, frowning over his glasses. "Is he Aiden Black's father?"

"Uncle," Dot said. "Lives up at Oakwood Nursing Home now. He's my age. I went to school with the ol' chap."

"There's your first lead, Julia," Jessie said, suddenly sitting up in her seat. "The poor girl's boyfriend's uncle owned the shop. If he didn't do it, he must know something."

Julia laughed stiffly as she looked around the room, but the group was not laughing with her; they were looking at her with the same serious expression as Jessie.

"What makes you think I'm investigating this?" Julia said, squirming in her seat. "This is one for the cold case team."

"If you say so, love," Dot said with a shake of her head as she stood up and collected their empty cups. "If you say so."

Roxy and Johnny caught each other's eyes for a moment before looking awkwardly back at Julia.

"What?" she protested.

"Well, your gran is right," Roxy mumbled, standing up and grabbing her coat from the back of the chair. "You're like a dog with a bone. You've always been the same way."

"Remember when Sammie Carlton stole my bike in Year Eight?" Johnny asked as he joined Roxy in standing. "You didn't stop until you found it. You interviewed everybody who was around the bike shed until somebody gave you a lead, and then you stood on the corner of Sammie's street and waited until you saw him with a bike so you could take a picture on your gran's camera. You spent your pocket money having the roll developed, just so you could go to the head master with proof to get my bike back. You've been the same ever since. I can't even count how many articles I've written recently where I've had to decide if I'm going to mention that you outwitted the police once again. If anyone can solve this, it's you, Julia."

"I'd rather not have that pressure," Julia said uncomfortably, her thoughts turning to Evelyn. "It happened twenty years ago."

Roxy and Johnny exchanged the same sceptical look again as they pulled on their coats. Dot appeared from the kitchen with a tin of biscuits, but rolled her eyes and retreated when she saw her guests were leaving.

"I'm not investigating this," Julia said with an awkward laugh as she caught Jessie's disbelieving gaze. "I mean it."

Jessie rolled her eyes and shrugged as she reached out for one of the clippings to look down at Astrid's face.

"It's cute that she thinks that, isn't it?" Roxy asked, slapping Johnny on the shoulder. "I give it a day."

"I give it an hour," Johnny replied with a wink. "I better get back to the office. This is the biggest story we've had in a while, and I want to make sure the team understands the sensitivities of it."

"I should get back to school," Roxy said as she checked her watch. "My lunch break is nearly over, and I'm behind on the syllabus after we shut early yesterday."

Her two friends left, leaving Julia alone with Jessie while Dot washed the cups in the kitchen. Julia read over the article of Evelyn pleading for information about her daughter's disappearance. She tried to put herself in the woman's shoes, but she could not even begin to understand her pain.

"Let's go," Julia said, already standing up. "I want to make sure somebody is there for Evelyn."

Jessie nodded her agreement, and they slipped out of Dot's cottage before she could force them to stay for another cup of tea. Julia had hoped she would be able to slip across the village without being seen, but as she looked across the village green towards her café, she knew that was going to be impossible. Word of the discovery had spread quickly around Peridale, and it seemed that every resident in the village had come out to see with their own eyes if it was true.

"The TV people are here," Jessie mumbled, nodding to a van adorned with a satellite dish. "They'll probably want to talk to you."

"Good luck to them," Julia said as they walked around the edge of the village green. "I don't want to talk to them."

Fruit Cake and Fear

They approached the crowd in front of her café, who were being held back by blue and white crime scene tape and uniformed officers. A white tent had been erected at the entrance of the alley where Julia's brand new bike was still in the back yard. Through the window of the café, she could see right through the beaded curtain to the men in suits in her kitchen.

"*Julia*!" Shilpa, the owner of the post office, cried. "We've just heard!"

"Is it really *her*?" Amy Clark, the church organist, asked, as she plucked a small bobble off her pale pink cardigan. "They won't tell us anything."

"It's awful, either way," Malcolm Johnson, the president of the Peridale Green Fingers whispered, his large frame looming over the crowd. "She was the same age as my Chloe."

"Just awful," Mary Potter, the owner of The Comfy Corner, sniffled as she dabbed her nose with a handkerchief. "She was *such* a lovely girl. Worked some Saturdays at my restaurant. How did you find her?"

All eyes in the crowd turned to Julia. She looked around the sea of faces, and out of the corner of her eye noticed somebody pointing her out to a woman who was being followed by a man clutching a giant camera. Barker slipped out of the white tent, and she hurried forward to catch his attention.

"The damn cold case team!" Barker cried as he ducked under the tape. They walked away from the scene and rounded the corner of the post office where he leaned against a red phone box. "This is *my* village, and they're not letting me anywhere near her. Acting like they're all high and mighty, but I just want to help. Happy to use my officers for crowd control, but won't tell me what's going on." Barker paused and inhaled before looking down at Julia. "Why is it always you, eh?"

"She was there before it was my café," she said, her brows tensing. "The storm knocked over a tree and – it doesn't matter. Has anyone spoken to Evelyn yet?"

"They haven't officially identified the body," Barker said, glancing over his shoulder and towards Evelyn's B&B. "But from what people are saying about this girl, how can it be anyone else?"

"I'm pretty sure it was her," Julia said. "She was wearing her Head Girl badge."

Julia looked towards the B&B, her heart stopping when she spotted Amy Clark scurrying towards it, her pastel pink cardigan and pale blue skirt sticking out. Leaving Barker leaning against the phone box, Julia set off at a run after her.

"*Amy!*" she called. "Where are you going?"

Amy turned around and glanced at Julia, but she continued on towards the B&B, not stopping until she was unclipping the garden gate. She shuffled down the path and yanked on the metal chain next to Evelyn's door. The musical doorbell chimed out around the B&B as Julia followed Amy up the garden path.

"Somebody needs to tell her," Amy muttered over her shoulder as she fiddled with the buttons on her cardigan. "It's better it comes from a familiar face than a man in a suit."

"They have people trained for this," Julia whispered, glancing at the police station across the road. "Please, this isn't –"

Before Julia could finish her sentence, the door burst open, the strong scent of incense hitting them both in the face. Amy coughed and wafted at the dusty cloud of smoke with a hand. Evelyn appeared through the smoke, the sweet and spicy burning sticks in each of her hands.

"*Amy! Julia!*" she exclaimed as she wafted the sticks around her head. "What can I do for you? I'm just showing my new guests one of the rituals I picked up during my travels in India three winters ago."

"They've found her, Evelyn," Amy blurted out, her cheeks burning red. "They've found her."

Evelyn's arms dropped to her sides. Just from how quickly every muscle in her face sagged, Julia could tell the B&B owner knew exactly who Amy was referring to.

"Found who?" she asked with an uneasy smile. "I'm quite busy, so if you –"

"*Astrid*," Amy said quickly, the name jumping out of her mouth. "Julia found her in the basement under her café. Didn't you, Julia?"

Amy nudged Julia in the ribs with her elbow and nodded at Evelyn. Julia opened her mouth to speak, but she did not know what to say to the woman who was pleading with her eyes to deny Amy's crazy tale.

Instead, all Julia could do was nod. She looked pathetically down at the floor and watched as the incense sticks tumbled from Evelyn's hands and sizzled against the carpet. With the weight of ten men, Evelyn dropped to her knees and let out the deepest and most painful moan the village had ever heard. Julia could not hold back her tears.

CHAPTER 4

Julia felt like a spare part in the days following the discovery of a body underneath her café. With the forensics team still combing over the building, she was not allowed anywhere near, so she stayed home, pacing back and forth in between bursts of nervous baking.

"What are you working on?" Jessie asked as she wandered into the kitchen.

"Another version of my mother's fruit cake," Julia said as she sieved flour into the bowl. "Since my birthday cake is currently going mouldy in the café's fridge that I'm not allowed to touch, I thought I'd make it again so you can at least try it."

"I still haven't tried all of these yet," Jessie said as she opened the fridge to point out the half a dozen other cakes Julia had baked so far. "With you in here and Barker tapping away in the dining room on that stupid typewriter, I feel like I'm going crazy."

"Why don't you go and see Billy for a couple of hours?" Julia suggested. "I'm sure he'll keep you entertained."

"He's gone down to the coast with his dad," Jessie said with a sigh as she looked down at her phone screen. "He can't seem to get a signal. He tried video calling me earlier, and I couldn't tell what was a pixel or a nostril."

Jessie tossed her phone onto the counter and doubled back to the bathroom. She closed and locked the door, only to scream and rip it open.

"He's done it *again!*" she cried. "*Barker!*"

Julia followed Jessie into the dining room. Barker's fingers were typing at lightning speed, the old keys clacking loudly against the paper. He rolled onto the next line and gulped down some cold coffee without looking up.

"*Huh?*" he said as he carried on typing.

"Is it *so* difficult to put the toilet seat up when you go?" she cried. "Or at least *wipe* it? I lived on the streets, and even *I'm* not an animal!"

"Mhmm," he mumbled as his typing sped up. "*Sure.*"

"And your underwear!" Jessie cried, her arms flapping. "Why is it *so* difficult to put them in the washing basket? You put them *next* to the washing basket, but never *in* the washing basket." Jessie paused for breath and folded her arms against her chest as she waited for a response. "Are you even *listening* to me?"

"Washing basket," he said with a nod, not taking his eyes away from the paper. "Gotcha."

Jessie grunted and turned on her heels, her face bright red.

"You deal with him!" Jessie snapped, looking Julia dead in the eyes. "Because if I don't walk away, I'm going to bash his head in with that bloody machine!"

Jessie stormed out of the dining room and into her bedroom, slamming the door behind her as she went. Julia inhaled and forced a smile as she tried to remember what it was like being a teenage girl full of hormones.

"Barker," Julia said softly as she approached him. "I know you're trying to catch up on those pages you lost, but Jessie has a point. This is her home, and you need to be a little less – *messy*."

"I'm not messy," he shrugged, finally looking up from the page. "And I'm not catching up, I'm starting again. Everything that is happening right now has just inspired me to write. My house being destroyed, the body under your café, it's all great material! There are so many more interesting cases to write about other than the Gertrude Smith one."

"I thought they were still shutting you out of the case?"

"They are," Barker said, after gulping down more cold coffee. "Which is what makes it so interesting. I get to fill in the blanks of what I don't know. My creative juices are flowing, and I need to get it all down on paper before I explode."

"Perhaps you should lay off the caffeine for a while?" Julia suggested as she picked up the cup. "Just lift up the toilet seat, okay?"

"I thought I did," he mumbled as he began to type again. "I'll try."

"Don't try," Julia said as she walked away. "Just do it."

Fruit Cake and Fear

After washing the coffee cup and hiding the jar of coffee in Mowgli's food cupboard, Julia continued working on her cake, only to be interrupted by a knock at the door seconds later. She listened out and waited for a moment until it became obvious nobody else was rushing for the door. Sighing to herself, Julia yanked off her apron and dumped it on the counter.

"I guess I'll just get it," she called out as she walked down the hallway towards the door. "It's not like I'm doing something."

Pushing forward a smile, Julia checked her reflection in the mirror and dusted the flour out of her hair before pulling on the door. Her smile quickly dropped when she saw who was on the other side.

"Alistair?" Julia exclaimed, her head recoiling. "What a surprise."

"I hope you don't mind me showing up like this," the old man said as he leaned his entire body weight onto a twisted wooden cane. "I suspect you've been expecting me."

Julia stepped to the side and let the man in. It had crossed her mind to speak to the man who had sold her the building that was now a crime scene, but she had not expected him to turn up on her doorstep. In any other scenario, she would have hunted him out immediately after finding the body, but she had been sitting on her hands, if only to prove to Roxy and Johnny that she was not the dog with a bone they insisted she was.

"Can I get you some tea?" Julia asked as the old man hobbled into the sitting room, the top of his back completely hunched as he used the cane like a third limb. "Or maybe some cake? I have a fridge full of the stuff."

"Peppermint and liquorice, if you have it?" he said as he lowered himself into the armchair next to the roaring fire. "I recall you offering it to me when we had our meetings about the building, and I rather liked the taste."

Julia retreated to the kitchen and quickly made two cups of tea. Even though he had not asked for some cake, she plated up two generous slices of Battenberg, if only to get rid of the products of her nervous baking.

"I tried to call ahead, but I think your mobile telephone number has changed," he said breathlessly as he leaned his head back against the headrest. "I don't remember that walk up your lane being quite so long."

Julia smiled sympathetically as she placed the

cake and tea on the table next to the chair. She cast her mind back to the last time she had seen him. It was on the day he handed over the keys, and even though he had not been a spring chicken, he had not seemed so frail.

"How are you?" Julia asked, perching on the edge of the couch. "You look – well."

"You shouldn't lie to an old man," he said through a shaky smile. "I'm riddled with arthritis, my blood pressure is haywire, and I'm recovering from a stroke I had before Christmas. Haven't been the same since, but they look after me up at Oakwood. I'm grateful for you buying my shop every single day because I wouldn't be able to afford that place otherwise."

He rested his eyes for a moment and seemed to be drifting off to sleep, but they quickly shot open, and he began to rub his swollen knuckles. Julia sipped her tea and waited for the old man to speak again.

"I wanted to come and see how you were," he started after taking a shaky sip of the tea himself. "I wanted to come the second I heard, but I've been full of a cold all week and today is the first day I'm feeling like myself. When I heard about Astrid, you were the first person I thought of."

"I'm okay," Julia said, not wanting to let him know she had not been able to shake the image of Astrid's skeleton from her mind. "It's Evelyn I'm concerned about."

"Ah, yes," Alistair said with a nod. "The girl's mother. How is she?"

Julia had not seen Evelyn since she had helped her up off the floor of her hallway. After settling her in her sitting room and shooing the guests back up to their rooms, Evelyn had turned and kicked her out. She had not been seen in the village since, although officers had been spotted going in and out of the B&B.

"She's holding up," Julia lied. "As well as can be expected."

"Twenty years is a long time to hold out hope," he said heavily. "I couldn't imagine being in her shoes, but I understand loss. My Mildred died last year. We retired up to Oakwood together, and it's not been the same since she left me. We never had children, so I gather it will be a different kind of loss, but a loss all the same."

Julia nodded and took a small bite of the cake. She thought about the questions she had been wanting to ask Alistair in the last couple of days, but now she was face-to-face with the man, she was not sure he would hold up to intense questioning.

"Do you have any idea how she got down there?" Julia asked, deciding to cut to the chase. "I never even knew there was a basement under the building."

"It was my workshop," he explained, his swollen hands resting on the chair arms. "I made my toys down there. Everything in my shop was hand carved by me, and I did a roaring trade until about thirty years ago when everyone started playing computer games. Nobody wanted what I had to offer, but I hung on for as long as I could. Finally shut up the shop in July of 1997. It was painful, but I knew I was doing the right thing. Rented the place out. It was taken over by a travel agent, and then one of those mobile phone shops, but neither lasted long. Didn't suit the village and what people wanted. It was empty for three years before you came back home. People said the building was cursed because nobody could succeed there, but you proved them wrong. Maybe I was the curse, or maybe – just maybe it was real after all, considering what has come to light."

Alistair paused to carefully lift his tea to his lips again. Each movement looked painful, but he pushed through. He set the cup on the table again and turned to Julia.

"I suppose you want to know why I paved the yard and hid the door to my workshop?" Alistair asked with a sad smile.

"The question did cross my mind."

"I wish I had an answer for you, dear, but I don't. I didn't pave the yard," he said with a heavy sigh. "When I closed down my beloved toy shop, I stayed away from the building. It was too painful. I regret to say I never went back out into that yard after my last day of trading. You don't have to do landlord inspections with those franchised businesses, you see. You know they'll look after it. By the time I sold it to you, the whole thing had slipped my mind. I didn't think anything of it."

Julia took another bite of her cake as she mulled over what Alistair had said. If he had not been the one to pave over the yard it meant anyone could have done it, and that was why they had got away with it for so many years. She quickly turned her attention to the flickering fire, forcing her mind to stop piecing things together. She reminded herself she was sitting this one out.

"Put channel three on," Barker said, storming into the sitting room. "I've just had a text from someone at the station. Oh – *hello*. I didn't realise you had company."

"This is Alistair Black," Julia said. "He's the man who sold me the shop."

"Ah, okay," Barker said with a nod as he shook the frail old man's hand. "It's a pleasure. Detective Inspector Barker Brown."

The old man smiled politely as Barker sat next to Julia and grabbed the TV remote from the table. He turned it on, and the screen of the *Pretty Woman* DVD menu from the night before lit up on the television. He quickly set it back to the digital channels and flicked through until he landed on the one he wanted.

"That's my café," Julia said, surprised to see a female news reporter standing on the edge of the village green. "What's going on?"

Barker shushed Julia and turned up the volume as he moved in closer to the TV.

"It's been three days since a body was found in the basement of this café behind me in the Cotswold village of Peridale," the reporter chimed monotonously as she read from a paper in her hands. "As suspected, we now have official word from the police that the body *is* that of missing girl, Astrid Wood, who vanished from this very village twenty years ago. Sources close to the victim have said she disappeared on the night of her high school prom and was never seen again until the recent storm, which was a knock-on effect from Hurricane Jessica over in the States, disrupting this small picturesque village to reveal a basement that has lain hidden for more than twenty years."

"So, it's official then," Alistair said with a solemn nod after Julia took the remote from Barker to mute the channel. "I don't know if I was hoping it would be another girl, not that it would make things easier, but my nephew has been in bits since hearing about this."

"Aiden?" Julia asked.

"They were an item," Alistair said. "So in love. Grace, Aiden's wife, is torn up too. She was Astrid's best friend. I used to call them the Three Musketeers. Aiden never stopped talking about her. He did everything he could to keep her memory alive, even if it was just in his own home. He's still got a picture of her on the mantelpiece. Never stopped hoping she'd come home one day, but we all knew that wouldn't happen."

"I'd like to speak to Aiden," Julia thought aloud, not realising the words were leaving her lips until it was too late. "I did find her, after all. It might provide him some comfort to speak to me."

Fruit Cake and Fear

"I think he'd like that," Alistair said as he forced himself out of the chair. "I should be going. It's pill time in twenty minutes. It's all fun and games when you get to my age, dear."

Julia helped Alistair out of the chair and handed him his cane. Not wanting to let him walk all the way to the nursing home alone, she called and paid for a taxi, and sent him on his way with the rest of the Battenberg cake to share with the other residents.

"You want to speak to Aiden?" Barker asked with an arched brow. "I thought you were leaving this alone."

"I am," Julia insisted. "But I'm involved whether I like it or not. I *did* find her body, Barker. Wouldn't you want to look that person in the eye if you were Astrid's boyfriend from twenty years ago?"

Barker opened his mouth to object, but he knew she was right. He retreated into the kitchen, no doubt looking for the coffee. When he did not find it, he sulked back into the dining room to continue with his furious typing.

Julia had thought confirmation that it was Astrid's body would bring her some peace, but it did not. It still did not explain how she had ended up underneath the café, or who had paved over the basement door.

Reminding herself of the promise she had made to prove Roxy and Johnny wrong, she continued measuring out the ingredients for the cake and pushed Astrid to the back of her mind.

CHAPTER 5

J ulia strolled into the village the next morning with her finished fruit cake in hand. Milky clouds blocked off the sky above, bringing a chill to Peridale. It signalled the end of summer and the imminent beginning of autumn.

She approached her café and looked through the dark window from behind the crime scene tape. The white forensics tent had been removed, allowing her new bike to have been returned to her, but she had been instructed to stay away from her café until they were finished with their examination of the basement.

"It's such a shame," Shilpa, the owner of the post office, said as she watered the flower boxes under her shop window. "Do you have any idea when you'll be reopening? I miss your cakes."

"Soon," Julia said with a forced smile. "I hope."

Julia left her empty café and set off up to the road towards Evelyn's B&B. It began to softly rain as she passed The Plough. She paused and looked up at the sky, regretting her decision to leave her umbrella at home.

"That's her," Julia heard someone whisper. "She's the one who found her."

Julia turned to the group of elderly women who were sitting under a parasol at one of the tables outside of the pub. She spotted Amy Clark amongst them, but she refrained from looking in Julia's direction. Julia gritted her jaw, wondering why she was being diplomatic, but she shook her head and continued on her journey to the B&B. The village was going to gossip about her regardless, and she would only add fuel to the fire if she commented. She had wanted to give Amy Clark a piece of her mind ever since she had ruthlessly broken the heart-breaking news to Evelyn, but she was waiting for the right moment; this was not it.

Leaving the old women to gossip, Julia approached Evelyn's front door, where the sign in the window had been switched to '*NO RESERVATIONS*'. Julia yanked on the chain, the musical doorbell ringing throughout the cottage. Julia had come prepared to be ignored entirely, so she was surprised when she heard footsteps heading towards the door, and even more surprised when a tall, slender man answered it.

"Hello?" he said, brushing his shaggy blond hair out of his face as he stared down at her. "Are you one of the guests?"

Julia smiled awkwardly at the man. Despite looking like a Kurt Cobain tribute artist, he appeared to be a similar age to Julia. He had red circles around his eyes as though he had recently been crying and Julia detected a faint scent of unwashed and twice-worn clothes.

"Aiden?" she mumbled, squinting at the man's face. "It's Aiden Black, isn't it?"

The man stared down at Julia with an arched brow for a moment before snapping his fingers together and flashing her a smile.

"Julie? The cake lady?"

"It's Julia," she said, holding up the box. "But you're right about the cake lady part. I brought Evelyn something I baked. I thought she might like to see a familiar face."

"*You're* Julia," he said again with a firm nod as he hugged his jaw with his palm. "I didn't put two and two together. I remember you from school. You were in Year Eleven when I was in Year Nine. I remember you taking over a lesson of Food Technology when Mrs Hargreaves came down with the flu. When they said a woman called Julia found – found her under a café, it didn't click."

"I'm sorry for your loss," Julia said. "I can't imagine what you're going through right now."

"You'd think having twenty years to get used to things would make it easier, but it doesn't," he said blankly, his eyes glazing over as he stared down at the cake box. "I think you might have wasted your time, I'm afraid. We came down with the same intentions, but Evelyn is – well, you know – she's being *Evelyn*."

Aiden stepped aside to let Julia in. She kicked off her shoes, remembering how Evelyn liked to regularly shampoo her carpets. She placed them next to the burn marks from the fallen incense sticks, making a mental note to buy Evelyn a bigger doormat to cover them.

"We brought flowers, but it seemed to make her worse," Aiden whispered as they walked down the long hallway to the sitting room. "Threw them straight into the bin."

"Evelyn doesn't like cutting flowers. She thinks it's torture."

Aiden looked down at her with a smirk, which he quickly dropped when he realised Julia was not joking. They walked into the dark sitting room, the only light coming from small tea light candles circling the table Evelyn was sitting beside the bay window. Her grey hair flowed free, and she was wearing a black kaftan as she mumbled under her breath with her hands clamped to a crystal ball.

Julia recognised the woman with curly black hair sitting on the couch as Aiden's wife.

"She's been doing that since we got here," she whispered. "It's Julia, isn't it?"

"It is. You're Doctor Black."

"Please, call me Grace," she said with a polite smile. "I haven't seen you in my surgery for a while. Did that rash on your hand clear up?"

"Turned out I was allergic to pistachios," Julia replied as she rested the cake on the coffee table.

"What's she doing?"

"She said she's trying to contact Astrid," Aiden said, his tone disapproving. "I think that's all she's been doing since it happened."

"Poor woman."

"I know," Grace said with a heavy sigh. "We were so upset when we heard the news, but we can't even imagine what she's going through. If I lost one of my boys, I don't know what I'd do."

Aiden squeezed his wife's shoulder as Grace dabbed at the corner of her eyes with a shredded tissue.

"I remember you all being friends," Julia said, recollecting everything Roxy and Johnny had reminded her of. "The Three Musketeers according to your uncle."

Grace looked up at Aiden. They shared a sweet smile before they both began to cry. Julia almost wished she had not said anything.

"Sorry," Grace said through her tissue with a strained laugh. "It's been twenty years, but we never gave up hope."

Julia glanced at Evelyn and noticed that her eyes were now open. She stared down at the crystal ball, but she appeared to be looking right through it.

"*Hope*," Evelyn croaked, her eyes wide and

unblinking. "I always had hope that my daughter would walk through that door one day with amazing stories of the life she had experienced away from this village. My hope is dead."

Julia suddenly looked down at the floor, guilt flooding through her. Would it have been better if she had never found Astrid? She hoped her guilt was misplaced, but Evelyn was a shadow of the woman who had handmade her a birthday card and forewarned of a storm.

"At least we have some closure now," Aiden said hopefully, even if his twisted expression said something else. "We won't go on wondering forever."

"I liked wondering," Evelyn snapped, suddenly turning and facing them. "I never dared search for Astrid's spirit because I could sense she was still out there somewhere, but I was wrong. Now that I'm looking, I can't find her. I cannot *connect*! They won't even let me see her body."

Julia refrained from telling Evelyn it was probably for the best that she did not see her daughter like that. She had not been able to shake the image of Astrid's skull staring back at her in the dark of the basement.

"We should go," Grace said, suddenly standing

up. "The kids are going to be driving Mark up the wall."

Aiden nodded his agreement, and they both headed towards the door. If Evelyn noticed they were leaving, she did not let it register on her face. Her hands slipped off the crystal ball, and she folded in on herself in the wicker chair.

"We shouldn't have come," Aiden said as Julia showed them to the door. "It was too soon."

"We've stayed away for too long," Grace added, grabbing her coat from the hat stand. "We visited all the time in the early days, but you know what life is like, especially when you have three kids to raise."

"I'm sure Evelyn understands," Julia replied with a polite smile. "She just needs time. Maybe try again next week. She'll get used to seeing your faces again."

"Are you staying?" Aiden asked as he pushed up an umbrella after peeling back the net curtain of the window next to the door. "I think it's going to take more than cake to get through to her."

"You'd be surprised."

After the couple left, Julia walked through to the kitchen and opened Evelyn's tea cupboard. She was faced with a dozen different varieties of tea in unlabelled plastic boxes. She opened a couple of the lids and sniffed the leaves, not wanting to pick one of Evelyn's illegal hallucinogenic teas by accident. When she detected what she was sure was green tea, she found a tea strainer in one of the drawers and prepared a pot.

With two plates, two forks, and a large knife, Julia carried the tray of tea through to the sitting room and set it on the coffee table next to Evelyn's ornate tarot card boxes. She sliced two generous helpings of the cake and placed them on either side of the table before pouring the tea into two cups. When she was satisfied, she walked over to Evelyn and rested her hands on the woman's shoulders, surprised when she let Julia lead her to the couch.

"A nice cup of tea and a slice of cake will make the world of difference," Julia said softly as she sat in the armchair across from Evelyn's sofa. "When did you last eat?"

Evelyn mumbled something and shrugged as she looked down at the cake. Julia picked up hers and demonstrated how to eat it. Like a child being taught for the first time, Evelyn copied and took a bite out of the cake.

"Delicious as always," she mumbled blankly as though it was an automatic response. "I don't know how you do it."

Julia swallowed her mouthful of cake before sipping the tea. She waited a couple of seconds to see if the tea had any ill effects, only taking another sip when she was sure all of her senses were still as sharp as ever.

"You can talk about her with me, but you don't have to," Julia offered kindly as she placed the teacup back on the table. "I was two years above her in school, but I talked to her."

"It's a small village," Evelyn said with a shrug, her eyes blinking slowly. "Astrid was all I had."

Evelyn feebly chewed another mouthful of the cake as though it were made from rocks and cardboard. She swallowed and let the plate slip off her knee and onto the couch.

"Was Astrid's father in the picture?"

"He died," she said bluntly. "Astrid was only a little girl."

"Oh, I'm sorry."

"Don't be." Evelyn slumped back into her seat and tucked her long wiry hair behind her ears. "He didn't know her, nor did he want to." Evelyn's eyes glazed over as she stared at the bright yellow teapot on the table, as though her mind was casting back to another time. "I was only sixteen when Astrid was born. I ran away from home and joined a commune in Liverpool. My parents were bankers. I wanted to be a hippie. I missed the movement, but there were still people out there living like that. The leader got me pregnant quite quickly. I didn't realise until it was too late that it was less of a commune and more of a cult. You know the sort. He thought he was God, and we were his to use. I got out before Astrid was born. That's when I found myself in Peridale. Father Patterson took me in and let me stay at the vicarage until I got myself on my feet. Worked as a shop girl at the post office until my mother and father died in a car accident. I inherited more than I deserved, so I bought this building and turned it into a B&B. I always loved having a house full of people, but maybe that came from my commune days. Turned out the commune was all a front for a drug smuggling ring and the leader, Saint John, as he liked to be called, was jailed. Cancer got him about thirty years ago. I only found out when I read about it in the paper. Astrid never knew him as her father."

"Did he know about her?"

"He fathered over forty children," Evelyn said with half a weary smile. "I doubt he knew a single one of them. I went to the funeral out of curiosity. It was pathetic. I was one of five people there. Two other women were from the cult, and the other two were women he'd been writing to from behind bars. I raised Astrid alone. I did the best I could, but I know people bullied her because I'm weird."

"You're not weird," Julia said quickly. "I don't think you're weird."

"You're too kind," Evelyn said with another half-smile. "You've always been so kind to me, Julia. I sense you're not a believer like me, but I feel the energies and spirits of the universe running through my veins like you feel your blood, which is why I don't understand why Astrid has never come through in all of these years."

"She will."

"What if she doesn't?" Evelyn said, suddenly sitting up, her hair springing from behind her ears and hanging over her eyes. "What if she blames me? I tried my best, but what if I wasn't enough for her?"

"You can't think like that."

"Well, I do."

"I don't think she got into that basement by accident," Julia said, almost regretting the words as quickly as they left her mouth. "You're not to blame."

"The police won't say it was murder," Evelyn said, suddenly animated. She darted across the table

Fruit Cake and Fear

to grab Julia's hands, knocking over her teacup in the process. "But they're not ruling it out. You're a smart woman, Julia. You've done this before. You're the only one who can find out the truth about what happened to my baby."

"Oh, I don't know about –"

"*Please*, Julia," Evelyn said through gritted teeth as she squeezed Julia's hand. "Promise me you'll try. For me."

Julia's mind cast back to Johnny and Roxy, and how foolish she had been to force herself to take a back seat to prove a point to her friends. Looking into Evelyn's raw eyes, Julia knew the woman would not be able to rest until she knew what had really happened to her daughter, and if Julia could be the one to do that, it would help her sleep a little better at night knowing she had helped.

"I'll try," Julia said. "But I can't promise I'll figure it out."

"You will," Evelyn said as she let go of her hands. She leaned back in her seat and nodded her head furiously, her eyes glazing over as she fiddled with the hem of her black kaftan. "I know you will."

CHAPTER 6

Roxy and Johnny came around later that evening with two bottles of white wine and a large tub of chocolate ice cream; Julia was grateful for both.

"Cake for dinner?" Johnny exclaimed as he looked around the half a dozen untouched cakes on the table. "I'm not complaining about that."

"I've been nervously baking."

Fruit Cake and Fear

"Remember when you nervously baked two hundred scones before our final maths exam?" Roxy said as she unscrewed the lid on the wine. "I spent that time revising like a madwoman. You *still* came out with a better result than me."

The old friends sat at the table and began their first slices of cake in between sips of wine, both of which they all seemed to need. Julia hoped the wine would give her the courage to confess the promise she had made to Evelyn that afternoon.

"My mum found this in my old bedroom," Roxy said as she rummaged through her large handbag. "I went back to Hollins for my work experience when I was at college. I ended up working on the yearbook team again."

Roxy slapped the '*Hollins High School Class of 1997*' yearbook in between her chocolate cake and wine. Johnny instantly scooped it up and began flicking through the laminated sheets.

"I've been working on a story to summarise the history of this case, and there's definitely something weird going on," Johnny said as he adjusted his glasses. "Astrid was supposed to meet Aiden and Grace at the war memorial in front of the church. They waited about twenty minutes for her, and when she didn't turn up, they went to the prom without her."

"You're not one of those who still thinks Aiden did it, are you?" Roxy mumbled after taking a deep sip of wine. "He was never charged. The poor guy will be carrying that around for the rest of his life. I'm not surprised he moved out of Peridale. The fella can't even go to the shop without people pointing and whispering about him chopping Astrid up into little pieces."

"She wasn't chopped up," Julia corrected her.

"Well, you get my point." Roxy stretched back and yawned, tossing her bright red hair over her shoulders. "I'm so tired. This new school year has wiped me out. My new kids are nothing like my last lot. They're out of control."

"Are you allowed to say that about six-year-olds?" Johnny asked with a smirk as he picked at the corner of a slice of carrot cake.

"I am when they act like they were raised in the wild," Roxy said as she shoved Johnny's shoulder. "Is that a love bite on your neck?"

Johnny quickly popped his collar up, his cheek colour instantly darkening. Julia hid her face behind her wine as she stared at the purple bruise on Johnny's neck.

"I walked into a wall," he mumbled. "It's

nothing."

"That's a hickey!" Roxy cried, dragging Johnny's collar down. "I've had enough of them in my time to know what one looks like."

Johnny pulled his collar back up and fiddled with his bowtie, his cheeks turning maroon. He caught Julia's eyes, but he broke the gaze quickly. She chuckled behind her wine glass. When she had been investigating the Peridale Green Fingers members' deaths with Johnny the previous month, he had told her he had not been on a date since their coffee date over two years ago.

"I might be seeing someone," he mumbled through a mouthful of carrot cake. "It's early days, alright?"

"Not early enough for a snog on the neck," Roxy chuckled, jabbing Johnny in the ribs. "Are you at it like teenagers?"

"Inappropriate," Johnny mumbled, his cheeks darkening even more. "Can we just leave it?"

"Who is she?" Julia asked.

"Or *he*," Roxy said, nodding from behind her glass. "Some of us favour the same sex, after all."

"*She's* a woman," Johnny corrected her, his spine suddenly stiffening. "She's a police officer. Works at the station."

"Peridale station?" Julia asked. "What's her name?"

"Sarah," Johnny replied, still unable to meet Julia's eyes. "She's nice."

"Aw, our Johnny boy has finally got himself a girlfriend," Roxy said as she ruffled his dark curls. "I'm chuffed for you."

"Me too," Julia said, forcing him to look in her eyes. "I really hope it works out."

Johnny shrugged and picked up the yearbook again. He flicked through the pages until Roxy let the topic go, which happened when Julia topped up her wine glass to the brim.

"Did you find out anything else about Astrid in your research?" Julia asked as she cut herself a slice of Swiss roll. "I went to see Evelyn this afternoon. I found out quite a lot about her father."

"I always assumed Evelyn summoned the energies of the universe and created a baby on her own," Roxy said as she stared blankly at the cake in front of her.

"She was sixteen."

"Oh,' Roxy said, her eyes snapping to Julia. "And the father?"

"A cult leader," Julia said before sipping her wine. "Died in prison thirty years ago after being found out as a drug smuggler. Had forty kids, according to Evelyn."

"Wow," Johnny said, pulling a notepad from his canvas bag. "Forty, you say?"

"Don't include any of that in your article," Julia said, pointing across the table. "She told me that stuff in confidence."

"But –"

"That wasn't a question."

Johnny sulked and slipped the notepad back into his bag. He picked up the yearbook again and flicked through the pages once more.

"I found out that Aiden got blind drunk at the prom," Johnny said as he landed on a picture of the Class of 1997's group shot, which was missing Astrid. "That was one of the reasons the police questioned him, because if he did chop her up into little pieces – *Sorry*, Julia. Don't give me that look! It is hard to break twenty years of stories you've heard. If he *did lock her in a basement*, he might have forgotten all about it."

"I think he had his stomach pumped that night," Roxy said as she looked down her nose into the glass of wine. "That's what I heard at least. Apparently, the police handcuffed him to the bed and questioned him there."

"Do you believe everything you hear on the gossip circuit?" Julia asked with a roll of her eyes.

"Most of it," Roxy said with a shrug. "Heard Barker had moved in with you after that storm knocked out his cottage."

"I heard that too," Johnny said. "Everyone was talking about it in The Plough last night. You'd think it was 1917, not 2017 the way some of the old biddies were talking about you living out of wedlock."

"It's only temporary."

"So, it *is* true," Roxy said with a grin as she slapped Julia on the shoulder. "That's a huge step."

"I couldn't see him on the streets."

"What's it like living with a man?" Roxy asked, her finger circling the glass. "Because Violet is as messy as any man. She doesn't put her underwear in the washing basket, she just –"

"Leaves it on the floor next to it?" Barker said, finishing the sentence for Roxy after appearing in the doorway, still in his trench coat and clutching his briefcase. "I heard I did that too. Are you the same, Johnny? I didn't even realise this was a thing."

"I live alone," he said meekly as he fiddled with his glasses. "I haven't noticed."

"Thank you!" Barker said, pointing at Johnny

with a grin. "We just don't notice these things. Maybe it's Jessie with the problem."

"I heard that," Jessie cried from the sitting room. "And you're the one with the problems. *Plural*."

"How was your day at work?" Julia asked, offering a seat to Barker.

"Stressful," he said. "The cold case team is using the station as their base of operations, but they're still not letting me in. I hear bits and pieces but nothing I can use."

"Use?" Roxy asked, leaning back in her chair, and arching a brow. "Are you going rogue?"

"He's writing a book," Julia explained, glancing at the typewriter in the corner of the room. "A crime novel."

"You write?" Johnny asked, narrowing his eyes on Barker. "I never knew that."

"It's just a hobby," Barker mumbled as he walked forward to grab the plate with the leftover chocolate cake on it. "I'll leave you guys to it. I'm going to take this and put my feet up in front of the TV."

Barker quickly kissed Julia on the top of her head before bowing out of the room and half closing the door behind him. The trio stayed in silence until the sound of the TV floated through from the sitting room.

"Writing a book," Roxy said, looking intrigued as she nodded her head back and forth. "That man is full of mysteries."

"I always thought he was gay," Johnny said bluntly as he forcefully flicked through the pages.

"Well, your gay-dar is well and truly broken because you never realised *I* was gay until the whole village found out about Violet," Roxy said, shoving Johnny's arm. "But, maybe you hoped he was."

"What's that supposed to mean?" Johnny snapped.

Roxy snickered behind her glass as she glanced at Julia with arched brows. Julia knew what her friend was implying, and it was not that Johnny had wanted Barker for himself, but rather hoped that Barker had wanted someone else so Julia was still free for his taking, not that she would have ever let that happen.

"Why is it when I get you two in a room together I feel fifteen again?" Julia sighed.

"Thank God we're not still fifteen," Johnny mumbled after sipping his wine. "Acne, awkward voices, arms too long for our bodies, bad fashion, bowl-cut hair."

"Speak for yourself," Roxy said, tossing her red

hair over her shoulder. "I was a fashion icon."

"I don't think tracksuit bottoms, neon yellow trainers, crop tops, and a frizzy ringlet perm made you a fashion icon," Johnny scoffed. "It's safe to say Astrid and her friends were just as awkward looking. Looks like they went on that same school trip to the lakes that we went on."

Johnny turned the book around to point out a picture of the trio in the corner of a double page spread dedicated to school trips. The trio stood in front of a lake, with Aiden in the middle. He was shirtless and had the exact same shaggy blond haircut he still sported. Astrid stood on his other side, her black hair over her face. Unlike Grace who was wearing a hot pink frilly bikini that exposed her midriff, Astrid was dressed head to toe in heavy black clothes with her arms tight across her chest.

"I don't think she was one for swimming," Roxy said as she squinted at the picture. "Is Aiden still sporting his Nirvana fantasy look?"

"The very same," Julia said. "Although Grace looks different. I forgot she used to be a blonde."

"I think she wanted to be Baby Spice," Roxy said after another sip of wine. "We all get to that age where we can't be bothered with the upkeep of dying our hair every four weeks."

"I don't remember you being a natural flaming red," Johnny retorted under his breath. "It was always more carrot than fire."

"Red is easy when you're already orange," Roxy said, shoving his shoulder again. "Going from black to blonde isn't. I'm not surprised she keeps it natural now."

Julia took the yearbook from Johnny and looked closely at the picture by the lake. Beneath the hair, Astrid looked so much like her mother that she was not surprised Roxy had thought it had been an immaculate conception.

"I told Evelyn I was going to look into things," Julia finally confessed, avoiding her friends' eyes. "She was trying to contact Astrid through a crystal ball. She worked herself up into such a state. She's going to suffer until somebody gets to the bottom of it."

Johnny sighed, and Roxy cheered. She held out her hand while Johnny dug in his pocket to pull out a twenty-pound note. He slapped it into her palm before she tucked it into her bra.

"Johnny thought you might *actually* sit this one out," Roxy said proudly with a wink. "I knew better."

Before Julia could question her friends for

placing bets on her, raised voices drifted in from the sitting room. After a final sip of wine, Julia pushed herself out of her chair and slipped through the door.

"What's going on?" Julia asked as Barker and Jessie fought over something on the couch.

"Barker won't let me watch what I want to watch!" Jessie cried, tugging on the remote control. "*Get off.*"

"I was watching the news," Barker snapped back, tugging on the remote. "You weren't even watching TV when I came in!"

"And now I want to!"

They both yanked on the remote control, neither of them letting go. Julia walked around the couch towards the television, reached behind it, and yanked the plug out of the wall.

"Now neither of you get to watch TV," Julia snapped, standing in front of the dead screen with her arms crossed against her chest. "You're far too old to be acting like this."

"She's not."

"He's ancient."

"Can't we all just get along?" Julia pleaded.

"No," they replied in chorus.

Julia sighed and rubbed her temples at the side

of her head. Without the retreat of her café, she had been forced to spend her days pacing around her tiny cottage, which might not have been so bad if Jessie and Barker did not erupt into an argument about something trivial every time they were in the same room.

"If you want the news, read the paper," Julia said, picking up the latest copy of *The Peridale Post* from the coffee table and tossing it to Barker. "And Jessie, you can borrow my laptop and watch something online in your bedroom."

"Whatever," she mumbled, jumping up from the couch and pulling her hood over her hair. "I'm going to Dolly and Dom's."

Before Julia could stop her, the front door slammed, and a frosty silence fell on the cottage. Barker leaned back in his chair and exhaled, wincing hard as he rubbed his stubbly jaw.

"It's been a stressful day," he said with a heavy sigh . "I'm sorry."

"It's not me you need to apologise to," Julia said softly. "It was her home before it was yours. You need to learn to live together in harmony."

"Hopefully it won't be for much longer," Barker said. "I've got the builders checking out my cottage tomorrow, so I should have some quotes to figure out how much that mess is going to cost me to clear up."

"Am I that bad to live with?" Julia asked, resting her weight on her left hip as she crossed her arms again. "I'm sorry I offered."

"It's not that," Barker said, grabbing her hand and pulling her into his lap. "I feel like I'm getting under both of your feet. Even Mowgli hasn't come near me since he's noticed I'm here every day."

Barker rested his finger under Julia's chin before kissing her softly on the lips. She did like having him around more often, but she had not expected it to disrupt the harmony of the house so much.

"We're going to go," Roxy said. "Places to be."

"Yeah," Johnny mumbled. "Thanks for the cake."

Julia pulled away from Barker and stood up. She brushed down her dress and smiled awkwardly at her friends as she showed them to the door.

"I left the yearbook for you," Roxy said as she opened her handbag to drop something large wrapped in a napkin inside. "I hope you don't mind, but I'm taking some carrot cake for Violet. She loves the stuff."

Julia kissed them both on the cheeks and waved them off as they both climbed into a taxi. When

Julia closed the door, she rested her head against the wood and inhaled, glad of the peace and quiet for a moment.

"I'm going to have a shower and get out of these clothes," Barker said as he walked to the bathroom. "I've already sent a text to Jessie to apologise, and she's – *Oh*, she's just replied. *Wow*. I don't know what this specific string of Emojis mean, but I don't think it's good."

"She'll adapt," Julia said, kissing Barker once more. "It's just been the two of us for so long now. She needs time."

Barker sighed as he stuffed his phone into his pocket. He loosened his tie as he walked into the bathroom, locking the door behind him. The second Julia was alone, Mowgli trotted out from her bedroom with sleepy eyes. She scooped him up and took him into the kitchen to feed him.

After clearing the wine and cakes from the dining room, Julia made herself a refreshing cup of peppermint and liquorice tea before sitting at her counter to pour over the yearbook.

She turned to the double page spread of formal school portraits, finding Astrid's under '*Head Girl*', which was next to Aiden's '*Head Boy*' spot at the top of the page. She traced her finger across the pale girl's face and sighed.

"How did you end up in that basement?"

CHAPTER 7

J ulia spent the next morning scrubbing her entire
cottage clean. When every surface sparkled, and
the fumes of bleach were starting to get to her
head, she rode her bike into the village for some
fresh air. She passed her gran's cottage just as she was
closing the door behind her, wearing the most
peculiar outfit.

"Some of the girls and I have joined a rambling

club," she exclaimed as she adjusted her waterproof coat. "I'm about to go on my first ramble."

Dot fiddled with the two metal walking sticks, the metal water bottle and compass on her belt rattling together. Dot joined or started a different club every month, but this was one of only a few that had come with an outfit.

"You look prepared," Julia said, suppressing a grin. "Rambling anywhere fun?"

"The countryside," Dot snapped, wafting her hands in the direction of the sprawling green fields surrounding Peridale. "I don't know, love. Between you and me, I'm already starting to regret joining, but Amy said it was fun. There was a good deal on this stuff in the catalogue, so it would have been rude to turn it down. When are you getting your car back?"

"I'm not sure," Julia said, her heart fluttering at the thought of her poor crunched up Ford Anglia. "The man at the garage said it would take a while to find the right parts because she's vintage."

"Well, I hope it's soon," Dot said as she peeled back her raincoat to glance at her watch. "You look funny riding around the village on that thing. I must dash."

"You   look   rather   funny   yourself," Julia

mumbled under her breath. "Have fun, Gran."

"Oh, do you think you'll be going past the doctors on your travels?" Dot asked as she unclipped her gate. "I need to pick up my repeat prescription for my blood pressure. I'm down to my last two pills."

"I don't think I —"

"Thanks, Julia!" Dot exclaimed as she plodded away, her various new accessories rattling and clanging. "You're a star."

Julia rolled her eyes as she remounted her bike. She headed the opposite way than her gran, avoiding looking in the direction of her café. She had called the police station again, just as she had every morning since discovering Astrid, but they were still being as vague as ever.

"You'll know when we know," the desk sergeant had said. "There's no need to call every morning."

Julia also avoided looking at Evelyn's B&B as she rode past. It had only been a day since she had promised to look into things, but she had not discovered anything yet, despite spending the previous night digging through every internet article she could find on the disappearance.

By the time Julia reached the top of Mulberry Lane, her calves burned, so she was grateful when she saw the doctor's surgery without a line of people outside it. She leaned her bike against the wall and walked into the small reception area.

A couple of people were sitting in the waiting area, nodding their acknowledgement to her, and a couple more began to whisper behind their hands. Julia did not need to overhear them to know what they were saying.

"I'm here to pick up Dorothy South's prescription," Julia said as she handed over her driving licence as identification. "I'm her granddaughter."

The young woman behind the desk smiled politely as she glanced over the ID before quickly handing it back. She typed something into the computer before digging in a drawer under the desk for the signed repeat prescription. Julia accepted it gratefully and thanked the young woman before turning around to head for the door.

"Julia?" a voice called from one of the doctor's offices on the side of the room. "What are you doing here?"

Julia turned to see Doctor Grace Black smiling at her from the doorframe of her office. Her black curls were tucked neatly into a bun at the back of her head, and she was wearing a stylish ruffled white blouse with pinstriped floor-length trousers that made her look exceptionally tall.

"I'm just picking up my gran's prescription," Julia said, holding up the green slip. "Don't worry, I'm in good health."

Grace looked down the line of people who were undoubtedly waiting to see her. She glanced at the small silver watch on her wrist before pushing forward a wide smile.

"Can I have a quick word?" Grace asked, smiling apologetically at the elderly woman in the chair nearest the door as she let out a loud huff. "I won't take up too much of your time."

Julia nodded before following Grace into her small office. It looked like a doctor's office should, with various health warning posters cluttering the room, a desk with a chair on either side, an examination table with a retractable blue curtain in the corner, and a full-scale skeleton on a frame. Julia gulped at the sight of the bones, hoping they were not real. She had seen enough skeletons to last her a lifetime.

"Take a seat," Grace said, pointing at the chair opposite her desk as she sat behind her computer. "I just wanted to ask you if Evelyn got any better after we left? We both feel terrible about the state she was in. We couldn't help feeling to blame."

"It's a tough time for her," Julia explained in a low voice. "Don't blame yourselves though. She perked up a little when I managed to talk to her, but we all deal with grief differently."

"That's true," Grace mumbled, her eyes glazing over. "I can barely eat since we heard. I just can't keep anything down. Aiden is the same."

Grace glanced at a framed picture on the edge of the desk, which was angled so the patient could also see it. It appeared to be a family picture taken on holiday, featuring Grace and Aiden, along with the three boys Johnny had told her about. They varied in age, with the eldest looking to be at least twenty, the youngest around five, and the one in the middle in his early-teens. The eldest had Grace's black hair, while the others had Aiden's sandier hair.

"We took that in Scarlet Cove last year," Grace said with a soft sigh as she picked up the picture. "It was Aiden's idea to holiday in the UK, so we picked a small fishing village on the south coast. We usually go to Cyprus or Spain, but we had just as much fun there."

"You have a beautiful family."

"Thank you," Grace said with a soft smile. "Isn't it odd how time flies? It feels like only yesterday that we were in school, and this was my mum's office, but my Mark turned twenty a couple of months ago. I don't feel old enough."

"Well, you don't look old enough," Julia said with a small chuckle. "I've got Jessie, and she's just turned seventeen."

"I never knew you had a daughter," Grace said as she rested the frame back where it belonged.

"I'm her foster mother," Julia explained. "Well, not officially, but social services are slow to act. I'm as good as, though. She was homeless until I took her in at the beginning of the year."

"That's very noble of you," Grace said. "Mark isn't Aiden's real son, but he's been there for him since he was born."

"I didn't know that," Julia said, looking at the picture again, noticing even more how much Mark stood out with his dark hair amongst the other blond boys. "Does Mark see his biological father?"

"No," Grace said flatly, her eyes narrowing slightly. "I got pregnant while I was still in school. Too many drinks at a house party. You know what it's like to be a teenager. Hormones are blazing, and you do stupid things you regret instantly. He didn't want to be a dad when I told him, so we went our separate ways after school. I haven't seen him since, but we don't need him. I had a lot of help from my parents in the early days before Aiden and I officially got together."

"Must have helped having a doctor for a mother," Julia said, remembering the fact from her youth. "Doctor Gambaccini?"

"Alessandra Gambaccini," Grace said with a smile. "She retired. I took over her office after working my way up. She worked here for nearly forty years before she hung up her stethoscope. Lives up at Oakwood Nursing Home now."

"She must be proud that you followed in her footsteps."

"She is," Grace said with a sweet smile. "It wasn't easy going through medical school with a newborn. I don't think I could have done it without Aiden being by my side."

"I should probably get going," Julia said, suddenly remembering her bike leaning against the wall outside. "I don't want to keep your patients waiting."

"Will you give Evelyn my love?" Grace said as she opened her top drawer before pulling out a flyer. "Why don't you come to The Flying Horseman on Friday night? It's a nice little pub over in Burford. Aiden's band is playing there, and it would be nice to catch-up properly over a glass of wine. You should bring that hunky detective inspector I heard you were dating."

Julia looked down at the poorly designed flyer for Aiden's band, which was aptly called '*Nerveana – The Cotswolds' Best Nirvana Tribute Band*'.

"I'll try and make it," Julia said as she pocketed the flyer along with Dot's prescription slip, despite punk rock not being hers, or Barker's, cup of tea. "Hopefully Barker isn't working."

"No pressure," Grace said, turning her attention to the screen as she began typing. "Can you send Mrs Wainthropp in? I suspect her hemorrhoids have been playing up again."

Julia slipped out of the room and informed the elderly woman that the doctor was ready to see her. Mrs Wainthropp scowled at her as she stood up with the aid of her cane, wincing as she did.

Leaving Grace to get on with her job, Julia slipped out of the surgery, glad to see her bike exactly where she had left it. She squinted into the distance at her father's antique barn at the bottom of Mulberry Lane, surprised to see a familiar redhead walking towards her with a plastic bag.

"Fancy seeing you here," Roxy said with a grin as she kissed Julia on the cheek. "Just been having a catch-up with your dad. Gave me a nice little discount on some antique pictures for my downstairs bathroom."

"My gran made me pick up her prescription," Julia said, pulling it out of her jean's pocket along with the flyer. "Just spoke to Grace. She invited me to see Aiden's band on Friday night."

"*Nerveana?*" Roxy mumbled with a snort. "That's tragic. I wonder if he's still with those nerds from school. They would get up on stage at every school event. They had as much star quality as a dry piece of toast. Are you going?"

"I'm not sure yet," Julia said as she stuffed the flyer back in her pocket. "Maybe they can tell me some stuff about Astrid, that might help me piece things together."

"Their tongues might get a little looser after some alcohol," Roxy suggested with a grin. "That's a good idea. I bumped into Mrs Hargreaves in the supermarket last night after leaving your cottage. We talked about Astrid and she said that the girl was bullied."

"Mrs Hargreaves, the food technology teacher?" Julia asked. "I thought she would have been retired by now."

"She's getting on in years, but she's still there,"

Roxy said as they started to walk up the street with Julia pushing her bike. "I knew people used to tease Astrid about how odd her mum was, but the way Mrs Hargreaves was talking made it sound more serious."

When they reached the top of the street, Julia checked her watch before saying, "It's half past three. I wonder if she's still at the school."

"There's only one way to find out," Roxy said as she pulled her keys out of her pocket. "I'm parked around the corner. Your bike will fit on the backseat."

***

JULIA COULD NOT REMEMBER THE LAST time she had visited her old high school, but it had barely changed since her days walking the halls. Hollins High School had been built in the 1960s to combine the smaller high schools in the villages surrounding it. Its square grey concrete buildings with large windows looked just as Julia remembered, with the only visible change being the modernised logo.

"It still smells the same," Roxy whispered as they walked down the main pink-painted corridor towards the food technology classroom. "Does it feel smaller, or are we just bigger?"

"I think it's the latter," Julia replied, glancing at the displays of students' work on the walls.

They pushed through two heavy double doors and walked down three steps into the common area. It was filled with the same metal benches and tables, but there was now a roof above covering it, reminding Julia of the cold winter days shivering with Roxy and Johnny.

Without needing to speak, they walked automatically down the network of corridors towards the technology block. A group of teenagers hurried past, glancing suspiciously at the two women. The green and black blazer had been replaced with a black jumper with the modern logo on the breast; Julia preferred the blazer.

"I spent most of my time here," Julia said as they approached Mrs Hargreaves' door, the scent of freshly baked bread drifting through the partially open door. "It was my second home."

"Do we knock?" Roxy whispered back. "Do we even call her Mrs Hargreaves, or Jillian?"

"I can't call her Jillian. That would be like watching a dog walk on hind legs. It wouldn't feel right."

The two women shared a look before they pushed on the door and walked into the familiar long room. The six mini-kitchen booths were just as Julia remembered them. The counters, floor, and equipment were all different, but it was similar enough for Julia to suddenly be transported back to her teenage years. Food technology had been her favourite subject, and the one she was naturally good at.

Mrs Hargreaves shuffled out of the storeroom, examining a can of peach slices over the glasses on the end of her nose. She was a petite and slender woman who barely scraped five feet in height. She had bushy hair, which was always pulled back and secured in a puffy bobble at the base of her neck. Aside from her brown hair now having streaks of grey and her face having more lines, the winds of time had barely changed her.

"As I live and breathe!" she exclaimed when she looked up and caught Julia's eyes. "Is that Julia South I see before me?"

"The very same," Julia replied, unable to contain her grin. "It's good to see you again, Mrs Hargreaves."

"It's Jill to you now," she said, setting down the can on her desk before clapping her hands together.

Fruit Cake and Fear

"You look so grown up! How many years has it been?"

"Julia just celebrated her thirty-eighth birthday," Roxy announced, nudging Julia in the ribs. "She's getting old."

"I'll hear none of that, Roxy Carter!" Jill said, pointing a finger. "Don't think I won't put you in detention just because you're a teacher yourself now. What brings you girls here? I suppose this isn't a social visit?"

The three women drifted over to the table where students would work on their written work after cooking and baking. Jill brought over a freshly made lemon drizzle cake, along with three cups of tea.

"Best part of the job," Jill said. "A girl in Year Ten baked this, and she's almost up to your standards, Julia. I haven't had a student as talented and dedicated since you. Sure, there have been gifted bakers, but nobody has matched you."

"She runs her own café," Roxy said, winking at Julia. "Best cakes in Peridale. She's famous around the village."

"I'm glad to hear it," Jill said as she sliced up the cake. "Last I heard you were working in a factory in London. I couldn't believe you were wasting your talent doing that."

"She followed a man to the big city," Roxy said, her tongue drifting across her lips as she reached out for a slice of cake. "She finally came to her senses, divorced the pig, and now she's dating a detective inspector."

"Technically, *he* divorced me," Julia mumbled before blowing on the hot surface of the tea. "But he did me a favour."

"You're better off alone, if you ask me," Jill said. "Mr Hargreaves is nice enough, but I'm sick and tired of picking up his underwear. He puts it *next* to the washing basket –"

"But never in it?" Julia interrupted.

"You have the same problem, then," she said with a roll of her eyes. "Sometimes I think they're all the same. How about you, Roxy? I forgot to ask when I saw you in the supermarket last night."

"Erm, I'm dating," Roxy said casually as she wiped the cake crumbs from her lipstick. "This *is* really good lemon drizzle cake."

"I heard you were a lesbian," Jill said bluntly before sipping her tea. "Isn't it funny how gossip travels?"

"She's called Violet," Julia said, suppressing a grin. "They're very much in love."

"I'm glad to hear it," Jill said with a firm nod.

"Too many people are judgemental these days. I'm happy to hear that you've been accepted."

"Well, there was one woman who tried to blackmail us before I told everyone the truth," Roxy mumbled from behind her cup, glancing at Julia. "But, she's dead now. My sister killed her. It's a long story."

"Ah, I heard Rachel was in prison," Jill said before taking a bite of the cake. "That was a hot topic in the staff room at the beginning of the year. Family, eh? Full of drama, but you can't live without them. So, what's the real reason you're here, girls?"

Julia and Roxy looked at each other, both sipping their tea, neither of them seeming to know how to broach the subject. Despite being a similar age to what Mrs Hargreaves would have been when she had taught them, Julia could not shake the feeling that she was suddenly a student again and the woman in front of her was her teacher.

"It's about Astrid Wood," Roxy started as she picked at the leftover cake on her plate. "I know we spoke about her last night. You mentioned something about her being picked on."

"Terrible news," she said after exhaling heavily. "Such a terrible shame. Of course, I knew she would be dead. Teenage girls don't just go missing like that and turn up alive twenty years later. Somebody would have seen her. I pity the person who found her body. I don't suppose it would have been more than bones."

"Yeah," Julia mumbled, her cheeks burning. "I suppose it would have been."

"The poor girl wasn't just picked on," Jill said, her voice rising. "She was being targeted! *Bullied*! I tried to help, but she wouldn't tell me who was tormenting her. The poor thing was terrified."

"What did they do to her?"

"It was the usual stuff at first," Jill started, her brows tensing as she stared off into the middle of the table as her mind cast back. "They destroyed her school books, broke into her locker, pushed her into the walls, but it stepped up a notch in the months before she went missing. I found her in the girls' bathroom, sobbing on the floor. Someone tried to push her head down the toilet. Poor thing was soaked through and shaking. Wouldn't tell me a thing! I always wondered if the people targeting her were behind what happened to her, but I didn't have any evidence. I told the police everything I knew about the girl, but they thought I was making it up. She never reported anything, and neither did I. It was in the days before bullying was taken as seriously as it is now. Back then, it was just brushed under the carpet. I should have filed a complaint with the head master at the time, not that he would have listened. He was a misogynistic pig!"

"Mr Hunter?" Roxy jumped in.

"That was his name!" Jill said, nodding heavily. "I did a little dance when he was fired. It was a couple of years after your girls' time, but he started turning up to school drunk. Punched a little Year Seven kid square in the face during break time after he refused to stop playing football. Instant dismissal, of course, but you can see why he wouldn't have taken me seriously about Astrid. Nobody would have. Evelyn insisted on burning sage all over the school before her daughter's first day. We all thought she was loopy. She'd flounce in on parent's evening in her kaftans and turbans and would give a crystal to all of her teachers. She was nuts, but I loved her. I still have those crystals at home somewhere."

Julia patted her pocket. She had been carrying the sapphire stone around with her since her birthday.

"And you have no idea who was targeting her?" Julia asked. "Anything you know might help."

"There was a popular group of girls at the time,"

Jill said as she tapped her finger against her chin. "Their leader was called Becky. I pulled her aside after a lesson once and asked her if she had been picking on Astrid, but she flat out denied it, and I was inclined to believe her, but I could have been wrong."

Julia took a bite of the lemon drizzle cake. It was light and fluffy, and had just the right amount of zesty lemon. Julia made a mental note to bake one when her café reopened.

"Is there anything else you might know?" Roxy asked. "Anything at all? Julia has promised Evelyn she's going to try and find the underlying cause of things."

"Why would you go and do that?" Jill asked, shaking her head at Julia. "Leave it to the police."

"Julia is quite the dab hand at solving murders," Roxy said quickly before Julia could say a word. "She's been cracking cases all year. She's got quite the reputation in the village."

"I have been reading about an awful lot of murders in Peridale recently," Jill said, her eyes glazing over again. "I'm afraid I don't know anything else. Well, there was that – *no*, I shouldn't say. I did promise her I would take it to my grave, and I haven't told a soul since."

Fruit Cake and Fear

Julia and Roxy glanced at each other, and then at their former teacher. They both shuffled forward on their chairs and leaned in across the table.

"Mrs Hargreaves, if you're keeping a secret for Astrid, she's been dead for over twenty years," Julia said. "You can't betray a dead girl's confidence."

"It's Jill," she said with a stern smile. "And I wouldn't feel right."

"You said you liked Evelyn, right?" Julia said, her voice beginning to shake. "I promised her I would figure out what happened to her daughter. Someone murdered Astrid and locked her in a basement. *I* was the one who found her. She was under *my* café. I *need* to figure this out, for Evelyn's sake. The poor woman is torn up."

Jill opened her mouth to speak before sighing and leaning back in her chair. She pulled off her glasses and cleaned them on the edge of her cardigan before sliding them back up her nose. She looked at Julia and smiled softly.

"You're just as feisty and determined as I remembered," Jill said, her smile growing. "I always loved that about you. I'd never met a student so determined to figure out why a recipe wasn't working before you. You never gave up until you had things figured out."

"Just tell her what you know, Mrs Hargreaves," Roxy pleaded. "She's going to figure this out one way or another, but wouldn't you rather be the person who helped, rather than the person who stood in her way? She was your best student, after all."

Jill turned to Roxy, her smile growing even more.

"You haven't changed either," she said with a small shrug. "I'm not surprised you became a teacher, Miss Carter. You were always a natural leader. I'll tell you what I know, but I can't promise it's going to mean anything, or help you in any way."

"Thank you," Julia said, edging forward even more. "Any little detail helps."

Jill exhaled heavily, pushing her glasses up her nose as she glanced up at the ceiling. For a moment, Julia thought the teacher was going to clam up, until she looked down, her eyes connecting with Julia's.

"It was in November 1996," Jill started, resting her hands together on the table. "I remember because there was snow on the ground and we had a particularly bad winter that year. I was on break time duty in the yard behind the science block. I usually got out of doing that job, but they always put more of us out there when it's snowing because you know what the kids are like. You'd think they had never seen snow before. I'd just finished telling some Year Eleven boys to stop throwing snow at the Year Seven girls outside the music classroom. Astrid was coming out, and I could tell she had been crying. I thought it had something to do with her clarinet lesson, but she told me she didn't go. I told her that her mother wouldn't be happy because she had paid for the term up front, and Astrid was such a gifted clarinet player. She asked if she could speak to me in private. You can usually tell when there is something seriously wrong with a student, or when they're just upset because they've fallen out with their friends, I could tell there was something seriously wrong. I knew she was in a relationship with the head boy at the time. I can't remember his name, but he was a nice enough kid."

"Aiden Black," Roxy jumped in.

"Ah, that's right," Jill mumbled with a nod of her head. "I remember Astrid telling me they had got close during their music lessons. I think he was into his guitar at the time. I abandoned my post and took her into this classroom. There was a group of Year Ten students working on their coursework, right where we are sitting, so I took her to the storeroom. With all of the cans and bags of food in there, it is quite soundproof, but she still barely spoke above a whisper. She started asking me about if I had children, so I told her I had four girls. She was crying the whole time, and I could barely tell what she was saying, but she started asking about the actual pregnancy and if it hurt. At that point, I straight out asked her if she was pregnant, and she denied it. She told me she was asking for a friend, but I didn't believe her."

"Astrid was pregnant?" Roxy mumbled. "That doesn't make sense."

"If she was, she didn't carry the baby full term," Jill added quickly. "I kept looking out for her stomach to start growing, and it never did, so I just assumed she either got rid of it, miscarried, or she really was asking for a friend."

"Grace told me she was pregnant during school," Julia thought aloud. "Her eldest son, Mark, has just turned twenty, and she can't be any older than thirty-six."

"Grace Gambaccini was pregnant?" Jill asked, a brow arching. "She was never in my classes, but I don't recall her being pregnant either."

"She was," Roxy said. "I remember seeing her just after she gave birth on the high street with a pram."

"I'm not surprised she hid it," Jill said, leaning in and lowering her voice. "Her mother was quite strict with her. I once remember Grace's English teacher saying her mother grounded her because she got an A on her coursework and not an A*. I think she was a doctor and wanted Grace to follow in her footsteps."

"She was," Julia said. "And Grace did follow in her footsteps."

"I guess the tough parenting does work sometimes," Jill said with a casual shrug. "Although in my experience, it's the kids who are pushed the hardest who fall the most."

The conversation soon turned to trivial matters such as Julia's café and the recent bad weather, so the two women finished their tea and excused themselves, leaving Mrs Hargreaves to mark some coursework.

Once again, they walked through the corridors as though they were still students, and out of the front door. Julia almost took the path across the grass in front of the school to the bus stop where they would catch the bus every day after school with Johnny, but she quickly remembered they had come in Roxy's car.

"Astrid must have known about Grace's pregnancy," Roxy said as she fastened her seatbelt across her chest. "They were best friends."

"Grace spoke so fondly of her mother today, but the way Mrs Hargreaves spoke about her, you'd think she was the Wicked Witch of the West."

"Which makes it all the more plausible that Grace confided in her friend, and why she kept the pregnancy so secret," Roxy said, twisting her key in the ignition. "That's why Mrs Hargreaves didn't know. I doubt anyone did until she gave birth."

After a short drive, they were soon in Peridale and pulling up outside of Julia's cottage. She took her bike out of the backseat and promised to see Roxy soon. After waving off her friend, she pushed her bike around to her back garden and let herself in the back door.

"Barker?" she called out. "Jessie?"

When nobody replied, and only Mowgli popped his head out of the sitting room, Julia collapsed on the couch, put her feet on the coffee table and closed her eyes to enjoy her silent cottage. She loved having people around her, but a small part of her missed the days when the cat had been her only company.

CHAPTER 8

Julia's phone vibrated on her bedside cabinet, waking her from her slumber. She squinted into the dark, the LED display of her alarm clock blinding her. It was only a little after six.

Sitting up immediately, Julia snatched up her phone and pressed the green answer button before cramming it against her ear.

"Julia South?" the familiar voice whispered

down the phone. "I know it's early, so I'm sorry if I woke you, but I thought you would like to know that forensics have released your café. You're free to reopen."

"Today?" Julia croaked, as she rubbed her eyes.

"That's why I called so early," the desk sergeant chuckled. "I knew you would need some time to prepare those delicious cakes."

"Thank you," Julia croaked, the grin spreading across her face. "Thank you so much."

Julia hung up and tossed her phone onto the bed. She looked down at Barker in the dark, his mouth wide open as he snored softly. Mowgli crawled from underneath the bed and jumped up into her lap, purring as he nudged her chin with his head.

"Let's get baking, boy."

***

BARKER WAS THE FIRST TO WAKE AFTER Julia. He stumbled into the kitchen, yawning wildly as he attempted to flatten down his dark hair.

"Nervously baking again?" he asked as he squinted down at the line of finished cakes on Julia's counter.

Fruit Cake and Fear

"Even better," Julia said, unable to contain her excitement. "I'm allowed to reopen."

"Reopen the café?" Jessie mumbled as she too stumbled out of her bedroom, also attempting to flatten down her hair. "Today?"

"*Yes!*" Julia beamed. "I've baked a lemon drizzle, another of my mother's fruit cakes, a red velvet, two dozen cupcakes, and I'm working on Barker's favourite double chocolate fudge cake."

"You're nuts, cake lady," Jessie mumbled as she turned and headed to the bathroom. "Absolutely nuts."

Julia whipped up the chocolate buttercream with the electric mixer as excited butterflies circled her stomach. She paused to let Barker scoop his finger along the edge, which he gratefully plopped into his mouth.

"It's different."

"I added some orange zest," she said as she continued with the mixing. "I was feeling experimental."

"It's good," Barker said with a nod as he sucked on his finger. "Really good. You never disappoint. I should probably have a shower before –"

The sound of rushing water cut Barker off mid-sentence. He turned to the bathroom and let out a heavy sigh as he shook his head.

"She knows I have a job to get to, doesn't she?" Barker mumbled as he snatched up the kettle. "I should get to go first. I jump in and out. She spends half the morning in there, wailing like a cat."

As if on cue, Jessie's off-pitch singing drifted under the door with the steam. Julia smiled to herself. She never recognised the songs Jessie was singing, but they had become the soundtracks to her mornings.

"She likes to wake up in there," Julia said with a shrug. "Let her do her own thing."

"Maybe she should drink coffee like everyone else," Barker said as he checked the cupboards. "Where is the coffee? Do I need to buy some more?"

"I hid it in Mowgli's food cupboard," Julia said, tucking the bowl under her arm and grabbing the jar of coffee. "There's such a thing as too much caffeine, you know."

Barker took the coffee with pursed lips before getting to work making his own coffee. He also placed peppermint and liquorice teabags into two cups. After the kettle boiled, he filled the cups to the brim, and took his coffee and one of the cups of tea, dropping it off outside the bathroom on his way to the sitting room. Barker's silent gesture put a smile on Julia's face.

An hour later when they were all ready, Barker drove them and the half a dozen cakes into the village. When they pulled up outside the café, the blue and white police tape still cordoning it off, Julia suddenly felt nervous. Since she had first opened, the café had never been closed for so long; Julia fervently hoped the villagers had not forgotten about her.

After ripping off the tape, unlocking the door, turning on the lights, and placing her fresh cakes in the display case, Julia was relieved when her regulars began to pour through the door.

"Good to see you back open," Shilpa said as her eyes drifted over the cakes. "I'm trying to watch my figure. My sister, Diya, is getting married next month, and I have a beautiful sari in the back of my wardrobe that I fit into ten pounds ago, but, life is short."

"A slice of the red velvet?"

"You know me so well, Julia."

After serving Shilpa, Julia was not surprised to see her gran bursting through the door, with a copy of *The Peridale Post* tucked under her arm. Not seeming to remember that the café had even been closed all week, Dot sat at the table nearest the counter and began flicking through the newspaper.

"A pot of tea when you're ready, love," Dot called out without looking up from the newspaper. "And a slice of whatever is freshest. Johnny's article about Astrid's life has just come out. I've been dying to read it."

"Maybe not the most *appropriate* word to use," Jessie said as she got to work making the pot of tea. "Anything interesting in there?"

"It's the usual stuff," Dot said as she flicked to the next page. "The same information and the same pictures we all saw twenty years ago. There's a quote from Aiden here. He said, '*there hasn't been a day since Astrid went missing that I haven't thought about her, and that's not about to change. I want to see her laid to rest so she can find peace*'. I still think he did it."

"*Gran!*" Julia exclaimed.

"What?" she replied through pursed lips. "It's *always* the boyfriend. He might not have chopped her up into tiny pieces and stuffed her in the walls, but he did lock her under this shop, which, might I *remind* you, belonged to his uncle."

Silence fell on the café as the rest of Julia's customers busied themselves with their drinks and cakes, nobody quite able to look in Dot's direction. Julia knew it was because everyone, including herself, knew she was making a valid point, even if she did not mince her words.

Barker came in a little after noon for his usual Americano and slice of chocolate cake, and even he seemed to notice the stuffy silence in the café after Dot had decided to read aloud large chunks of the article, adding in her unique brand of commentary.

"Happy to be back open?" Barker asked as he peered through the cake display case, his eyes landing on the finished chocolate cake.

"Ecstatic," Julia snapped back with a strained smile as she glanced at her gran over his shoulder. "It's like I've never been away."

"Can we talk?" Barker asked, leaning in slightly. "In private."

Julia nodded and instructed Jessie to take over behind the counter. They walked through the kitchen and out to the yard, where the wall was still half-destroyed, and the stone slabs were still missing. The only sign that the police had even been there was the large clamp locking the basement door in place, which resembled a car wheel clamp.

"Because it's not my case, I don't feel like I'm breaking any rules telling you this," Barker said as he pulled the heavy back door shut. "I don't even know if it's true myself yet, so I'm only passing on a rumour one of the boys at the station overhead from one of the cleaners when they were cleaning next door to the investigation room the cold case team is working in."

"A rumour?" Julia replied, crossing her arms and leaning in. "About Astrid?"

"They're saying she might have died of natural causes," he said, his eyes narrowing slightly. "It's hard to determine a cause of death when you're dealing with a skeleton, but most unnatural causes of death tend to show up in broken bones."

"Natural causes?" Julia echoed, recoiling her head slightly. "What kind of natural cause?"

"That's all I know. Maybe she starved to death, or just died?"

"Sixteen-year-old girls don't just die," Julia replied with a huff. "And if it was natural, who went to the trouble of making sure nobody ever found the basement door?"

"Maybe the two events weren't linked?" Barker suggested. "Although that doesn't make much sense."

"None of it does. Alistair claims not to have known who paved the yard. He thinks it might have been the businesses that took over the shop after he closed up."

"Do you believe him?"

"I have no reason not to," Julia said with a shrug. "He's a nice old man. He came to see me, remember. I didn't even seek him out."

"The police have," Barker said with a dry smile. "I don't know what they wanted to talk to him about, but I doubt he told them anything more than he told you because he wasn't arrested or charged with anything."

Julia soaked in the new information. She glanced at the door, the image of Astrid still burned in her memory, where she knew it was likely to stay for the rest of her life.

"I need to speak to Alistair again," Julia thought aloud. "Maybe he'll remember something he doesn't think is significant, but it might lead me to the truth."

"I'm not even going to tell you to stay out of things," Barker said with a smirk. "The cold case team thinks they know everything, so it might be nice if you wipe the smiles off their faces by figuring it out first."

"A little old baker like me?" Julia replied, flipping her hair over her shoulder. "I don't know what you're talking about, Barker Brown."

Barker and Julia walked back through the

kitchen, giggling like school children, but that stopped the second they pushed through the beaded curtain and saw Evelyn standing in the middle of the café. Julia's smile quickly dropped, the tense atmosphere as thick as the storm clouds that started this chain of events.

"*Evelyn*," Julia said, pushing forward a smile. "It's good to see you."

Evelyn looked through her grey hair at Julia, and then around the room, but nobody dared meet her watery gaze. Even Dot sunk into her chair as she carefully closed the newspaper and flipped it over to the back sports page.

"*What?*" Evelyn croaked, the dozen crystals around her neck clanging together. "Why are you all suddenly acting different? She's been dead for twenty years. None of you cared last week."

There was an uncomfortable shuffle in the café, all heads bowing even lower, including Julia's. It had been so long since she had thought about Astrid's disappearance that she had almost disconnected it from the eccentric B&B owner she had grown to love.

"Why don't you sit down and I'll plate you up some cake?" Julia suggested, attempting to look into Evelyn's red raw eyes. "Does that sound nice?"

Fruit Cake and Fear

Evelyn opened her mouth to speak as she met Julia's stare, but no words came out. She looked around the café, all heads bobbing down again, before turning around, her black kaftan swishing behind her.

"I don't know why I came," she mumbled before storming out of the café.

The stilted silence remained for what felt like a lifetime. Julia looked down at the floor, remembering what she was standing on. Just like Astrid with Evelyn, she had somehow mentally disconnected the discovery in the basement from her café above it.

"Well *that* was *awkward*," Dot exclaimed, breaking the silence with a loud cough. "I must dash. I rather enjoyed my first ramble, so some of the girls and I are venturing out and taking on the Chipping Camden trail."

Dot scurried out of the café, leaving behind the newspaper. Julia stepped around the corner and picked up the latest edition of the paper. The headline '*ASTRID WOOD REMEMBERED*' jumped out, along with a picture of a younger Astrid grinning at the camera with a birthday cake in front of her.

Julia flicked through the pages, landing on a

double page spread of photographs detailing the story of what had happened. An old photograph of her café caught her eye, even though it looked completely different. The pale blue exterior and '*Julia's Café*' sign were gone, replaced with an exposed wood front, a window filled with hand-carved toys, and a '*The Toy Box*' sign above the door.

"It's quiet in here," Roxy exclaimed with a stilted laugh as she walked into the café. "Have I come at a bad time?"

"You've come at a perfect time, actually," Julia said, glancing at the clock. "You get forty-five minutes for your dinner, don't you?"

"I have forty-one of them left."

"Good," Julia said as she hurried around the counter to grab her pink pea coat. "Is your grandma still at Oakwood Nursing Home?"

CHAPTER 9

Oakwood Nursing Home sat on the outskirts of Peridale at the end of a winding country lane. The luxury residential care home was situated in the middle of the countryside, and there were no other signs of life for miles around. For those who had money in the village, it was the perfect place to retire.

"My grandma is lucky my granddad had a

decent life insurance policy," Roxy said as they drove past the lavish fountain in front of the entrance. "She would never have been able to afford this place otherwise. It's more like a spa than any care home I've seen."

"I've only been once," Julia said as Roxy pulled into one of the free spaces behind the 19th century manor house. "My gran blagged her way in and pretended she spoke German."

"Sounds like your gran."

"Nothing surprises me anymore. I'm just glad you know someone on the inside. I don't think I could fake my way through reception again." Julia said.

They walked around the side of the manor, the leaves crunching underfoot. Before they pushed on the heavy double doors, they both stared out at the sprawling countryside. Dark clouds stained the horizon like ink in water.

"The village looks so small from up here," Roxy said, pointing out a small cluster of cottages. "Puts things in perspective."

"It does," Julia agreed. "Somewhere down there, someone knows the truth about what happened to Astrid."

"Or someone in here," Roxy reminded her as

they turned to the door. "Let's hope Alistair doesn't press his panic button when he sees us."

They pushed on the doors and walked across the grand entrance hall, past the biggest bouquet of fresh white lilies Julia had ever seen. Just as she feared, the same young woman was behind the reception desk, reading a copy of Bram Stoker's *Dracula*.

"It's getting to the good part," the young nurse announced, holding her finger up as she finished the page. "He's just about to bite her and – *how* can I help you?"

She turned the page and marked her place with a cardboard bookmark with a pink tassel. She placed the dog-eared book on the desk and beamed up at them with her widest '*customer service*' smile. If she recognised Julia, she was not letting it register on her face.

"We're here to see Glynnis Taylor," Roxy said through a forced smile. "She's not expecting us, but I'm sure she won't mind her granddaughters popping in."

Roxy gave Julia a look that read '*play along*', sparking a dreaded feeling of déjà vu from her last visit.

"Roxy and Rachel?" the young woman said after typing in something on the computer under the desk. "Your grandmother is taking tea in the orangery." She finished typing and looked up at Julia before whispering, "Rachel Carter? Why does that name ring a bell?"

"No reason," Roxy said, linking Julia's arm and dragging her towards the door that admitted them entry to the home. When they were on the other side of the door, Roxy whispered, "Having a serial killer for a sister has many more downsides than you'd imagine."

"Have you been to see her since –"

"Since she stabbed Gertrude and William Smith?" Roxy jumped in, glancing at Julia out of the corner of her eye as they made their way down a long and beautifully decorated corridor. "I haven't. Mum has, but Rachel didn't talk much. She's convinced herself she's innocent. I might have been inclined to believe her if you hadn't been the one to pin the murders on her. It's just through here."

They walked through a door labelled '*Orangery*', down a small corridor, and out into a large glass conservatory, which looked out on a full-sized tennis court.

"Is that my Roxy?" a little old woman with large magnifying glasses called out, squinting across the room. "It *is*! Oh, no. What has happened now, chicken? The last time you came was when you told me about those awful things that crazy sister of yours did."

"Nobody else has died," Roxy said. "Well, not anyone we're related to. I promise it is just a social visit. You remember my friend from school, Julia?"

The little woman with white hair that had been rinsed orange squinted through her thick lenses at Julia, a small smile spreading across her tanned, wrinkled face.

"The cake girl!" Glynnis said with a snap of her bony fingers. "Of course I remember you! You're Dorothy's granddaughter. We went to school together. How is ol' Dot? Still running around the village pretending she's not on the slow decline to death?"

"Something like that," Julia chuckled softly as they took seats across the table, a spiralled tray of sandwiches and cakes in the middle of the table. "Enjoying your afternoon tea?"

"It's dry rubbish," she exclaimed loudly, glancing at one of the nurses who was standing on the edge of the room. "You'd think for the price we're paying they wouldn't try and fob us off with this packaged nonsense. They need to get you up here. I'm sure you could teach them a thing or two, that's if you're still baking."

"Julia has a café in the village," Roxy said after picking up one of the crust-less sandwich triangles. "She bought Alistair's old toy shop a couple of years ago."

"I don't get down there much anymore," she said after a sip of her tea. "There's no need. Everything I could ever want is up here, except for perhaps a *fresh* cake every now and then."

"I almost wish I'd brought something with me," Julia said as she glanced over the afternoon tea offering. "There's nothing worse than dry cake."

"*Finally!*" Glynnis exclaimed, slapping her hand on the table, rattling the teapot. "You'd think I was asking for them to move heaven and Earth. I can't tell you how many complaints I've stuffed in that suggestion box, but do they listen? Do they *heck*! My Albert didn't pay his life insurance promptly every month so that I would be forced to spend my twilight years eating dry cake."

Julia chuckled as she glanced at the nurse, who was smiling politely in a way that said she had heard it all many times, possibly every day. From what Julia remembered of Glynnis in her younger years, she had always been amusing.

"I suppose you've heard about Astrid Wood,"

Fruit Cake and Fear

Roxy said after pouring herself and Julia a cup of tea. "Julia found her."

"You did?" Glynnis gasped, her soft fingers resting on Julia's. "Oh, you poor girl. I can't imagine that's something that will leave you."

"They found her under Julia's café, which, like I said, used to be the toy shop," Roxy said as she circled her finger around her teacup. "Isn't Alistair a resident here?"

A wicked grin spread across Glynnis' face as she loudly slurped down her milky tea.

"You've always been the same, Roxy, my dear," she said as she set her tea down. "Even when you wanted me to give you money for penny sweets at the corner shop, you'd always ease your way into it. Not like that sister of yours. She would demand things. '*I want. I want*', was how most of her sentences started. And now look at her!"

"I don't know what you mean," Roxy said, her cheeks turning a similar hue to her hair.

"He's a resident," Glynnis said with a nod of her head. "Came up here after his wife passed away. It's not often the wife goes first, but cancer doesn't care what gender you are, does it?"

Glynnis glanced at Julia, and it seemed they were both thinking about Julia's mother for a second. Julia pushed forward a smile, not wanting her mind to wander back to that place.

"Is he around?" Roxy asked. "While we're up here, it would be nice to speak to him. Julia's quite the amateur detective these days, and she's promised Evelyn she's going to look into things."

"Batty Evelyn?" Glynnis asked, snorting with laughter. "She was here last month for a psychic night. Started predicting death for everyone. You don't need to be psychic to know our life expectancies are on the shorter side up here! The nurses had to ask her to perk up, but not until she started channelling dead relatives. Some of the old biddies lapped it up, but I saw right through her performance. She's a charlatan if ever I've seen one!"

"Grandma," Roxy said, laughing awkwardly, her cheeks turning an even darker shade of red. "The woman has just found out her daughter was murdered. Maybe you can be a little more sensitive?"

"I didn't live through the second world war to be sensitive, dear," Glynnis said, shaking back her white and orange hair. "When you get to my age, you'll realise there isn't a lot of time to be treading on egg shells. Say what you think, or don't bother talking."

"You sound just like my gran," Julia said.

Fruit Cake and Fear

"The difference between your gran and I is that I've *accepted* my age," she said, nodding around the conservatory, which was filled with elderly men and women, some of whom looked like they were narrowing in on turning one hundred. "The thought of her scuttling around that village exhausts me. If you want to speak to Alistair, he's usually hanging around the tennis court out there with Alessandra."

"Alessandra Gambaccini?" Julia asked, craning her neck to look at the tennis court. "Of course. Grace did mention her mother was a resident here."

"She's one of the younger ones," Glynnis said as she joined Julia in looking out of the window. "She's got some sense. Took her doctor's pension and put it to use. She's a spring chicken compared to most of us. Alistair dotes on her. The man is riddled with arthritis and has a bladder as weak as a pregnant woman, not that he'd know it. If that's the reason you girls came up here, you can go and play detective and leave me to enjoy my dry cakes in peace."

Roxy kissed her grandma on the cheek before they walked out of the open double doors, leaving Glynnis to get back to her afternoon tea. The sun peeked through the murky clouds above, the scent of incoming rain in the air. They walked over to the tennis court, where two women were battling it out, grunting and running back and forth across the court as though they were playing at the Wimbledon finals.

"There's Alistair," Roxy pointed out the man who was sitting on a cooler box, clutching onto a cane. "Is that Doctor Gambaccini? I hardly recognise her."

Julia squinted and looked at the woman on Alistair's side of the court, who seemed to be taking the match more seriously than her opponent. Julia only remembered Doctor Gambaccini from her younger years, as the change-over between mother and daughter had happened while she was living in London. From what she remembered of the doctor, she had been a stern woman without the warmth of her daughter. She had blonde hair, which had always been scraped back into a neat French roll, and Julia had never seen her not in a trouser suit. The woman in front of her had curly blonde hair, which moved freely in the wind as she darted for the ball with her racket, and she was wearing a skin-tight white vest and an above the knee tennis skirt, with white trainers and socks.

"Is it possible she looks younger now than I remember?" Julia said to Roxy. "She must be in her late sixties, at least."

"Suddenly those lines around my eyes feel a little deeper," Roxy whispered back. "How long do these matches tend to go on for? All I know is when tennis is on TV, all of my favourite shows get pushed out of the way."

They stood on the edge of the court next to a group of bystanders, who did not seem as interested in the game as the two women playing. Alistair was bobbing his head from side to side as he watched the ball go from side to side.

"*Out!*" he declared when the woman playing Alessandra missed the ball.

The two women shook hands over the net before retiring to their things on the edge of the court. Alessandra walked over to Alistair, who handed her a towel and a water bottle with shaky hands. When two of the elderly bystanders shuffled forward with their bags, Julia and Roxy took their opportunity.

"Great game," Roxy exclaimed, slapping Alessandra heartily on the back. "I'm the biggest tennis fan you'll meet, and you are up there with the best."

"Thank you," Alessandra said with an unsure smile as she dabbed the sweat from her forehead.

"Do I know you?"

"We're friends of Grace," Roxy answered before Julia could say anything. "We're visiting my grandma, Glynnis."

"I don't know her," she replied flatly. "Alistair, will you get off that box? I want a cold bottle of water. You've clutched this one so hard it's gone warm."

Alistair stumbled up, leaning his entire bodyweight on his cane. He stepped to the side, but when Alessandra did not lean in to open the cooler box herself, Alistair fumbled his arthritic fingers against the clasp while Alessandra checked her fingers, more interested in her chipped manicure than the struggling elderly man. Unable to watch, Julia opened the box for him and pulled out a cold water bottle. She passed it to Alessandra, who strained a polite smile, despite her eyes being empty.

"It's good to see you again, Alistair," Julia said, resting a hand on the man's shoulder. "How are you holding up?"

"Oh, you know," he mumbled through shaky lips. "One day at a time. Alessandra, this is the woman I was telling you about. The one who found poor Astrid under the toy shop."

"Oh," the doctor mumbled, her expression

suddenly softening. "I can't imagine that was easy."

"Everyone keeps saying that," Julia said with an awkward laugh. "It wasn't. Did you know her well?"

"She was my daughter's best friend," she replied as she twisted the cap off the plastic bottle. "We should move out of the way. They're about to start a new game, but I don't think you can call what they do tennis. I was just about to take a walk around the grounds. You girls can join me."

Julia and Roxy glanced at her, unsure if it was an instruction or a question. Alessandra did not wait for a response and strode off the court. The two women followed, smiling their apologies at Alistair.

"You say you know my daughter?" Alessandra said, inhaling the cool air as they set off down a winding stone path, which seemed to circle the entire grounds. "I dare say it's going to rain."

"We went to school with her," Julia said.

"Really?" she said curtly, looking them both up and down quickly before continuing with her walk. "You look *older*."

"Only a couple of years older," Roxy said through pursed lips as she glanced questioningly at Julia.

"Well, I don't remember you," she said with a small shrug as they passed under the shade of a large oak tree. "Do keep up. Your heart won't feel the benefit if you stroll everywhere like snails. Were you friends of that husband of hers?"

"We know him," Julia said, almost jogging to keep up. "Did you know Astrid well?"

"I told you, she was my daughter's best friend," the woman snapped, glancing over her shoulder to shoot a stern look at Julia. "That husband acts like he's still in school. He hasn't had a proper job since. Thinks that band is '*work*'. *Ha*! I'm sure he accepts peanuts as payment. It's a good job my daughter followed in my footsteps, or they wouldn't have a penny to their name. It's the kids I feel sorry for. What kind of role model is he? I told her not to marry him, but she always did have a thing for the charity cases. I always thought that was why she was a friend to Astrid. She felt sorry for her because of that mother of hers."

"Do you remember anything about when she disappeared?" Roxy asked.

"What sort of question is that?" she snapped, suddenly stopping walking, causing Roxy to bump into the back of her. "Everyone remembers that. We searched the village high and low for signs of her, but who was going to check a basement under a toy shop? I do feel for Evelyn, even if she is a little –

peculiar. Maybe it would have been better if she had never found out. I can't imagine she's in a good way right now."

"She's not," Julia said, frowning at the mean woman. "Your daughter seems very happy with Aiden."

"Does she?" Alessandra scoffed as she set off walking again. "If she hadn't just had the baby, I doubt they would have got together. It was their grief that pushed them into each other's arms, but the baby kept them together. He wanted to be noble, even though he wasn't the father."

"Isn't that an admirable quality?" Roxy mumbled. "I'm adopted. I had a great life."

"It's *idiotic,*" she said with a strained laugh. "And your situation was different. I remember your mother crying in my office about her infertility troubles. I was the one who suggested adoption in the first place. Aiden was just a child pretending to be an adult. They both were."

"But they *are* still together," Julia said, her tone growing increasingly frustrated. "That must count for something."

"If you say so," Alessandra said, glancing up at the darkening clouds as a drop of rain landed on her nose. "I'm going back inside before I get soaked."

Without another word, Alessandra began jogging back towards the manor, leaving Julia and Roxy to watch in shock.

"What an *awful* woman," Roxy mumbled.

"Awful," Julia echoed. "Let's speak to Alistair before it starts to –"

Before Julia could finish her sentence, there was a rumble of thunder, which was followed by sudden rain. It drenched them both through in seconds as they attempted to run back to the nursing home, the path nothing more than puddles underfoot.

Once back in the orangery, Julia and Roxy stood on the edge of the room, dripping from head to toe. Some of the elderly residents who had retreated inside at the first sign of rain stared at them with frowns and pursed lips. Glynnis shook her head as she bit into another slice of cake.

"If you're looking for Alistair, you're too late," Glynnis announced. "He's gone upstairs for a nap. Probably tired out from Alessandra working him out on that court."

When they were back in Roxy's car, they stared at the rain in silence as they shivered before setting off back towards the village.

"Something weird is going on," Roxy announced when she pulled up outside Julia's café as the rain began to ease off. "I'd love to discuss it more with you, but I've only got six minutes left of my lunch break, and I haven't eaten yet."

"I'll make you a sandwich," Julia said as she climbed out of Roxy's car. "On the house. I stole your break."

"I don't mind," Roxy said with a smile as she pushed her red hair out of her face. "It's rather exciting. I'm not surprised you get so involved in these things. My adrenaline is pumping."

Roxy walked into the café, but Julia hung back and looked at Evelyn's B&B at the end of the street. She owed it to the poor woman to figure out the truth, and soon.

CHAPTER 10

"And *breathe*," the antenatal midwife called out to the group. "In and out. Nice and slowly."

"This woman is bonkers if she thinks you can breathe your way through childbirth," the woman next to Julia and Sue whispered over to them. "This is my third, and you forget all of this when you get in there. Your primary objective becomes to kill the man that got you in this mess."

Fruit Cake and Fear

"It takes two to tango, darling," the man behind her said with an apologetic smile when he noticed the horror on Sue's face. "Is it your first?"

Sue nodded and rubbed her stomach. She looked back at Julia, fear in her wide eyes.

"Twins," she mumbled before gulping hard. "Is it really that bad?"

"Ask for the gas and air," the woman said with a knowing wink. "By the time it happens, you'll be too high to notice if it's one or two. Are you together?"

"We're sisters," Julia said, looking around the room and realising they were the only same sex couple. "The father had to take a late shift at the library."

"*Breathe in!*" the midwife announced. "And *out!* Remember, it's all in the technique. If you time your breaths right, it will be a walk in the park."

"More like a drunken stumble through a forest with a blindfold on," the woman next to them said. "Good luck to you."

When the antenatal class was over, Julia helped her pregnant sister off the ground. Over the last couple of weeks, her stomach had grown even bigger, and now there was no doubt that there were twins inside.

"They're the size of aubergines now," Sue said as they walked out of the village hall with the other soon-to-be parents. "Two *whole* aubergines. Neil said they're starting to recognise my voice at this stage, but I don't know what to say to them."

"I don't think they'll quite understand English yet," Julia said, linking arms with her sister as they walked towards Sue's car. "You'll be fine. I'm going to be with you every step of the way."

"Do you promise?" Sue mumbled, looking her sister dead in the eyes as the sun started to set on the village. "I'd be lying if I said I wasn't terrified, Julia. Maybe I shouldn't have waited until I was thirty-two. I was fearless in my twenties."

"It's just your hormones."

"*Hormones!*" Sue cried, pushing her caramel locks behind her ears. "You sound like Neil. '*It's your hormones, love*', he keeps saying. I dare any man to do this."

"I can't even imagine what you're going through," Julia said, her voice catching at the back of her throat.

"You will," Sue said, clutching her sister's hand. "You're not out of the game yet. Thirty-eight is young! Did you hear about those women who gave birth at seventy in India? There's still time!"

Fruit Cake and Fear

"*Seventy?*" Julia snorted. "I can't think of anything worse!"

"I saw a documentary about it at gran's last week," Sue said as she unlocked her car. "Who knew post-menopausal IVF was a real thing? I could see gran's eyes twinkling for a second, but I told her not to get any funny ideas."

"She'd do it just to break the record of being the oldest woman."

They climbed into the car and waited for the other cars to pull away. Sue closed her hands around the steering wheel and stared off into the distant setting sun.

"I don't want to go home and be on my own," she said, turning to Julia. "Do you have any ice cream in your freezer?"

"I've got a better idea," Julia said, pulling a crinkled flyer out of her pocket. "Didn't you used to be a fan of Nirvana?"

***

THE USUAL TWENTY-MINUTE DRIVE TO the village of Burford turned into a thirty-five-minute crawl, thanks to Sue's sudden regard for driving well under any given speed limit. By the time they pulled up in one of the few free parking spaces outside The Flying Horseman on the main road in the small picturesque village, Julia was surprised not to have missed the gig entirely.

"It's not The Plough," Sue mumbled as she climbed out of the car and looked up at the three-story red brick pub with rooms, which looked to be just as busy outside as it was inside. "I never thought this was your sort of thing."

"It's not," Julia said, pulling the flyer out to make sure she had the right date and time. "I never expected it to be so busy, considering it's a tribute band."

"I think they played at Neil's sister's wedding a couple of years ago," Sue said, linking arms with Julia as they crossed the road. "They were quite good. He's a good sound alike. This wouldn't have anything to do with you finding Astrid Wood's body, would it?"

"What makes you think that?"

"This is Aiden's band," Sue said as they approached the busy pub. "I remember them from school. They were above me by a few years, but they played in an assembly once."

The men smoking cigarettes outside of the pub all looked similar to Aiden, with scruffy clothes and shaggy hair, even if some of them were thinning out considerably, not that they seemed to notice. They pushed through the crowd and into the pub, the wall of sound hitting them immediately. Julia recognised the lyrics to *Smells Like Teen Spirit*, which she was sure was the only song she would know some of the words to all night.

They pushed their way through the crowd, which was significantly thicker than Julia had anticipated. When they were at the bar, she ordered orange juice for Sue, and a glass of wine for herself. After paying, they pushed their way back through the crowd to find a free spot to watch the band.

"*Julia!*" a woman cried over the music. "You came!"

Julia turned to see Grace sitting at a booth with the three sons she recognised from the photograph in Grace's office.

"Do we go over?" Sue said. "She's our doctor. She's been up close and personal *down there*. Isn't it weird?"

Ignoring her sister, Julia dragged her over to the table. Grace shuffled around, making room for them on the edge of the booth.

"I wasn't expecting to see you tonight, but I'm glad you're here," Grace said, the wine making her talk a little looser than she had in her office. "These are my sons, Mark, Joey, and Ben. Say hi."

Julia smiled at the three boys, but they grumbled at her. She caught Mark's eyes and noticed the black eyeliner lining his eyes. With his jet-black hair, electric blue nails, and studded leather jacket with a pink and yellow lightning bolt on the pocket, he looked like he belonged in a glam rock band. The younger two boys shared Aiden's blond hair and looked a little shyer in the pub surroundings.

"They don't usually let kids in this late," Grace explained over the loud music. "We know the landlord. He's a big fan of Aiden's band. Do you like it?"

"It's – *loud*," Julia said with an awkward laugh. "Sue was a big Nirvana fan in her youth."

"I think we all go through that stage," Sue said, rubbing her bump in time with the bass guitar. "Looks like Mark is going through it now."

Sue laughed at her own joke, but nobody else did. Mark's cheeks blushed, and he quickly hid his painted nails under the table. Julia smiled her apologies at the young man, before shooting her sister daggers.

"He does an excellent David Bowie," Grace explained, her wine breath hitting Julia's nostrils as she sloppily leaned in. "He usually gets up and does a few songs when his dad is finished, don't you, Mark?"

Mark nodded, but he could not have looked more uncomfortable if he had tried. Julia caught the boy's eyes again, and she was sure she saw him screaming for help. She wondered if he got up onto the stage by choice.

"You look so much like your dad," Sue explained, leaning in to look at Mark. "You have his nose."

Julia coughed uncomfortably as Mark's cheeks blushed even darker.

"He's not my real dad," Mark said, his voice deeper than Julia expected.

"He *is* your dad," Grace said, tapping him on the knee. "He's been there since day one, and that's all that matters."

"He doesn't know who his real dad is," Ben, the youngest, chimed in. "We think he was the milkman's. That's what grandma says."

Mark slapped his brother around the back of the head, which in turn caused Grace to slap Mark. Julia could see Sue had trodden on a sore subject, which Sue seemed to have a habit of doing, and was something that could not be blamed on her pregnancy.

Silence fell on the table as the music in the packed pub carried on. Julia glanced at the stage as Aiden did his best Kurt Cobain impression in his long-sleeved blue-striped t-shirt, with his blond hair stuck to his face as he sung his heart out into the microphone. Every vein in his bright red neck and face throbbed wildly, calling out for some release. When the song finished, the lights turned to black, and a CD took over while the band took a break.

A couple of minutes later, Aiden walked over, rubbing his face with a black and white bandana. When he noticed Julia and Sue sitting at the table with his family, he smiled curiously at them.

"Julia," he said as he patted her on the shoulder. "Good to see you. And this must be Sue. It's been a long time, but you look almost the same, just a little more – *pregnant.*"

"Is that code for fat?" Sue asked blankly, her expression dropping.

"Men, eh?" Grace said, laughing awkwardly. "Wouldn't know how to say the right thing if their lives depended on it."

Aiden laughed awkwardly as he turned to look at the bar. He motioned to the bartender to pour him a pint, before pulling a packet of cigarettes from his back pocket.

"I'm just going out for some fresh air," he said, tapping the box with his finger. "Helps with the vocals."

Aiden slipped through the crowd, leaving the rest of them in silence.

"Where's the ladies room?" Julia asked Grace.

"Just over there," Grace said, pointing in the opposite direction of the front door. "Next to the fruit machine. You can't miss it."

Julia shuffled past Sue and headed in the direction of the glowing fruit machine. A man covered head to toe in tattoos smashed one of the buttons with his fist and pound coins shot out of the tray at the bottom. Julia ducked behind the machine and smiled awkwardly at him for a moment before pushing her way through the crowd towards the front door, keeping herself as close to the bar as she could. After stepping on more than one persons' toes, Julia burst through the front door and into the fresh air, which was not so fresh thanks to the cloud of cigarette smoke.

"Didn't have you down as a smoker," Aiden mumbled through the half-finished cigarette dangling from his lip as he offered Julia the pack.

"No, thank you," she said as she joined him in

the amber glow of the streetlight he was leaning against. "I just came out for some air. It's a bit stuffy in there."

A cool breeze ran down the busy street, wafting Julia's hair across her face. She tucked it behind her ears and smiled at the man, who was almost a stranger to her, and yet she was linked to him in a way that words could not describe.

"How's Evelyn doing?" he asked. "I've been meaning to pop in, but the time never feels right."

"I'd be lying if I said she was doing better," Julia said, jumping out of the way as a rowdy group of young men made their way down the street, cans of beer in their hands and football shirts on their backs. "I've been trying to figure out what happened to Astrid."

"Are you a police officer?" he asked, his eyes squinting as he sucked on the cigarette. "I thought you were a baker?"

"I am," she said with an uncomfortable laugh. "I'm just asking around to see if I can uncover something the police might not know."

"They've spoken to me half a dozen times since you found her," Aiden said, his jaw gritting as he tossed the cigarette stub to the ground. "Feels like it did back then. They never believed a word I said then, and they don't now. They keep making me go over it, as though it's easy to remember exactly what happened twenty years ago. When it comes to that day, I remember every detail until I started drinking the whiskey at prom."

"What happened?" Julia said.

Aiden squinted down at her as he pushed his sweat-soaked hair away from his face. She could tell he was deciding if he was going to tell her everything he had told the police.

"It was the day of prom," he started. "Astrid made a big deal about not wanting to go. She said she couldn't find a dress, but I told her she should just go in whatever she wanted. I didn't care what she wore. We had a huge argument that morning at the B&B when I went to see her, and she said she wasn't going. I told her not to bother, and I left. That was the last time I saw her. I felt so guilty. I walked around the village for hours, before going to a phone box and using the last of the money I had from my Saturday shift at my uncle's toy shop. She didn't pick up, but Evelyn did. She promised me she would talk Astrid around. Said something about needing to realign her chakras. I don't understand all of that stuff myself, but Evelyn sells it well. I told Evelyn that I loved her daughter and that I was sorry for storming out. She thought it was the sweetest thing she'd ever heard.

"She wasn't like the other girls at school, she was different. She didn't dress the same, or act the same. She read old books I'd never heard of, and always came out top of the class. She liked old music and weird Middle Eastern food that I could never stomach. I fell in love with her the minute I spoke to her during a music class in Year Nine. People said it was puppy love, but I knew it was real. I still know it was real. It was as real as love gets between two people, which is why I would never do what people said I did to her."

Aiden paused to pull another cigarette out of the packet. Julia's mind pushed forward the rumour she had heard more than once about Aiden killing Astrid and chopping her up into little pieces. She could not believe anyone who had looked into the man's eyes when he was talking about Astrid would believe that.

"I waited at the war memorial with Grace. She was supposed to be going with this kid called Brandon, but he broke his arm that morning. I didn't know she was pregnant at the time, but she gave birth a couple of days later. She hid it so well. Had on a floaty dress. It was one of those under the ribcage babies. I didn't know that could happen, but she barely showed. We waited until the last minute before the prom started before leaving. I was going to visit the B&B, but all of the lights were turned off. I thought they'd both decided Astrid could do better than me, so I went to the prom without her. I nicked one of the teacher's hip flasks, and I got blind drunk on whiskey for the first time. Apparently, I disappeared and turned up back at the war memorial the next morning. Uncle Alistair found me and took me home, but I didn't remember anything until I woke up on his couch. Because I didn't remember a thing, people thought I was lying."

"Did you ever remember?" Julia asked him as he paused to light another cigarette.

He took a deep drag before blowing the smoke out of his nostrils. His eyes widened, and his jaw gritted tightly as he stared down at Julia with an intensity she had never experienced before.

"I don't remember a thing," he said darkly. "And I've had to live with not knowing for twenty years. The only thing I've had to hold onto is how much I loved her. I wouldn't have wanted to hurt a hair on her head sober, so why would I suddenly want to drunk?"

He stared imploringly at Julia, but she did not have an answer for him. As she stared into his sad eyes, she realised he was not entirely convinced that he was not the one to have locked Astrid in the basement.

"Aiden?" a deep voice called from the entrance of the pub. "You're back on."

Julia was surprised to see that it was Mark who had referred to him as *'Aiden'*.

"He's going through a phase," he explained. "I just wish it would end sooner rather than later. We thought he'd skipped the rebellious stage, but the second he turned twenty, it's almost like we got a new son entirely."

Aiden smiled at Julia as though to thank her for listening before slipping back into the pub. Seconds later, Sue burst through the crowd, twiddling her index finger in her left ear.

"There you are," she said, relieved when she spotted Julia. "Please, can we go? I can't spend another second with Grace. She's a completely different woman with some wine in her. Draped her arm around my shoulder and started showing me pictures of her new kitchen on her phone, then made me type in my social profiles so she could follow me on *all of them*."

Julia chuckled as she linked arms with her sister before they crossed the road. She thought about everything Aiden had told her, her stomach turning uneasily. She glanced back at the rowdy pub as the band started up again, the heavy guitars and drums spilling out into the streets.

"I still think Aiden did it," Sue whispered as they climbed back into the car. "I can tell you don't believe that, but sometimes rumours start somewhere."

"I'm not so sure anymore," Julia replied, not believing the rumours, but believing the unsure look she had seen flicker in Aiden's pained stare. "And I don't think he's sure either."

CHAPTER 11

After a slow drive back to Peridale, Sue pulled up outside Julia's cottage at the same moment it started to rain again.

"I've got that ice cream you asked about in my freezer if you want to come in for a scoop," Julia said as she unbuckled her seatbelt. "It's chocolate and cherry, your favourite."

"As tempting as that sounds, Neil will be

finishing work within the hour, and I want to wash the smell of other men and the pub off me."

"Good idea," Julia said, kissing her sister on the cheek. "I'm here if you need me for anything."

"I know," Sue said with a soft smile. "If you are investigating Astrid's death, just be careful."

"I'm always careful."

"No, Julia, I'm being serious," Sue said, her tone deepening. "Whoever is involved in this has been keeping the secret for twenty years, and I don't think they're going to give themselves up quietly."

Julia jumped out of the car and stood in the rain for a moment as she watched her sister drive away, her warning echoing around her mind. Was Julia really putting herself in danger? Deciding it was necessary if she was going to get anywhere near the truth, she unclipped her gate and hurried down the garden path.

"You *idiot!*" Barker's cry echoed through the cottage, greeting Julia as she pulled off her damp coat. "You've ruined the *best* chapter!"

"I was *trying* to be *nice!*" Jessie called back. "I didn't have to make you a coffee!"

"I didn't *ask* you to!"

"That's where the '*trying to be nice*' part comes in!" Jessie cried, her voice growing. "It wasn't even my fault. Mowgli tripped me up."

Julia kicked off her wet shoes and walked into the dining room. Barker was sitting behind his typewriter, with his papers spread across the table, most of which were now covered in black coffee.

"Can't I leave you two alone for five minutes?" Julia sighed as she rubbed her temples.

"It was an accident!" Jessie cried.

"Look at what she's done!" Barker cried even louder.

Julia picked up one of the soaked sheets and held it up to the light. Unlike the paper in Barker's destroyed cottage, the ink was still intact.

"Barker, this will dry," Julia said firmly. "Jessie, you know you need to look out for Mowgli."

"So, you're saying this is my fault?" Jessie asked as she looked down her nose at Julia. "I *knew* you'd take his side."

"I'm not taking anyone's –"

Jessie did not let Julia finish her sentence. She turned on her heels and hurried into the hallway. Barker dropped his head into his hands and let out a deep sigh.

"Jessie," Julia called into the hallway. "Let's just talk this through."

When Jessie didn't reply, Julia walked back into

the hallway, where Jessie was furiously tying the laces on her black Doc Martens.

"I'm going to Billy's."

"But it's raining."

"I don't care."

Jessie pulled the hood over her head, grabbed her keys from the side table and left the cottage, slamming the door behind her. The letterbox rattled, bringing with it another rumble of thunder. Julia ran to the door and pulled it open, but when she looked out into the dark rain, she couldn't see her young lodger.

"Jessie?" she called out, her voice drowned out by another rumble of thunder.

"She'll come back when she's ready," Barker said, appearing behind her to slip his hands around her waist. "You know what teenagers are like."

"No, Barker," Julia said, wriggling away from him as she closed the door. "I know what *you're* like. You're just as bad, if not worse. You're the adult in the situation. You should know better."

Barker frowned at her for a moment, and Julia almost expected him to launch into a rant to prove her point, but he exhaled and nodded his agreement.

"I'm sorry," he whispered, doubling back and walking into the sitting room. "It's been a stressful day."

"That's no excuse."

"I know."

Barker knelt on the hearthrug and began stacking logs in the fireplace, the wind whistling down the chimney. Julia watched him for a moment before joining in.

"What's happened?" Julia asked quietly, knowing the hard approach was going to get her nowhere.

"I got the quote back from the builder for my cottage. It's going to cost more than I have."

"How much more?"

"About thirty thousand more than I currently have in my savings," he said, a meek smile shaping his lips. "I knew it would be expensive, but I never expected it to be *this* expensive."

"Can't you take out a loan?"

"The bank isn't going to throw good money after bad. I took out a huge personal loan for the house. I had most of it saved up, but I wanted to buy it outright without any mortgages. I put almost every penny I'd saved up over my career into buying that place for my fresh start in the country, but I didn't expect it to literally crumble around me."

"You weren't to know this would happen."

"What idiot doesn't have home insurance?" he cried, rocking back onto his heels. "A stupid idiot who doesn't expect the worst, that's who."

"A loveable idiot." Julia rested her hand on the back of his neck. "What are you going to do?"

"Maybe rent somewhere until I can afford to fix it, or until some fool buys it off me to at least pay off my loan?" He chewed the inside of his lip, his eyes glazing over as he stared at the stacked logs. "Emily's place across the lane is still empty. I know she's trying to sell, but maybe she'll give me a six-month tenancy if I grovel enough?"

"You know you can stay here until you figure it out."

"Can I?" Barker said, letting out a strained laugh. "From where I'm standing, Julia, this isn't working out like we hoped. I knew it would take some time to adapt, but a day hasn't passed where I haven't argued with Jessie over something."

"So, stop arguing with her," Julia suggested, kissing him on the cheek. "She's a kid walking around in adult's shoes. She's been through a lot in her short life. She's more fragile than she lets people see. This is the first stable home she's had in her whole life, and now it's suddenly changed, and if I were to guess, I'd say she feels threatened."

"I never thought about it like that."

"That's why you have me to explain it," Julia said with a wink. "She just responds better to a soft approach. You know, she used to leave her underwear on the floor next to the washing basket too, but I asked her politely not to, and she never did it again."

"She's not the only one who needs to adjust," he said as he looked around the cottage. "I've lived like a bachelor for too long. I never realised how much work went into keeping a home tidy."

Julia stood up and ruffled Barker's hair. He got to work starting up the fire as the lightning flashed behind the curtains and thunder rumbled above. Julia pulled her phone from her pocket, scrolled to Jessie's name, and sent her two simple words: '*Come home*'.

CHAPTER 12

J ulia opened her eyes and looked into Mowgli's as he kneaded the creases out of the blanket. Blinking through her tiredness, she tickled the top of his head. He purred gratefully as he nudged her chin with his wet nose.

"How did we end up in here, boy?" she croaked, sitting up and nudging Mowgli down to her lap.

She looked around her sitting room. The

remains of the fire smoked in the grate. There was an empty bottle of wine and the DVD case for *Pretty Woman* on the hearthrug.

Julia tossed off the blanket and shuffled into the kitchen, still in the clothes from the day before. She quickly made herself a cup of peppermint and liquorice tea before feeding Mowgli. Hugging the hot cup, she stared out of the window at the milky sky above her garden.

"I dare say it's going to rain again," she said to Mowgli.

"You know talking to yourself is one of the signs of madness," Barker announced with a grin as he stumbled out of the bedroom in his underwear, scratching under his arm like an ape. "Is there any coffee?"

"I guess I am mad," she replied, pulling the jar from Mowgli's food cupboard. "I hid it from you again because I think you were overdosing on the stuff."

"Not possible."

"Seventy cups of the stuff will kill you."

"I'll try and not drink *seventy* cups." Barker kissed her on the head before taking the jar. "How did you sleep?"

"Fine," Julia said as she rubbed her neck.

"Although I think I might need a massage to work out these knots. That, or I buy a new couch that you can't feel the springs in."

"You looked too peaceful to wake."

"I don't even remember falling asleep."

"You were gone by the time Richard Gere snapped the jewellery box on Julia Roberts' fingers," he said as he scooped two generous heaps of coffee into a cup. "I was waiting for you to tell me that Richard Gere snapping the box was improvised, and her laugh was genuine. You tell me every time, so when I didn't hear it, I looked over and saw you had fallen asleep. I pried the wine glass from your fingers and put your favourite fluffy blanket over you."

"You could have woken me."

"I know, but you looked comfy." Barker filled the cup with boiling water. "Besides, it was nice to be able to starfish in the bed. I miss my super king."

"I'm sorry my peasant double bed is too small for you, my lord," she joked. "I'm going to jump in the shower."

Julia took her tea into the bathroom, locking the door behind her. She pulled the curtain across, turned on the shower, and sipped her tea sitting on the toilet lid while she waited for the water to heat up. When steam billowed over the top of the curtain, she undressed and jumped in the shower.

The hot water woke her, reminding her of what had happened the night before. She wondered if Jessie had snuck back in during the night, or if she had slept over at Billy's.

After shampooing her curly hair and washing her body, Julia jumped onto the bathmat. She tucked a towel under her arms, shivering in the chilly bathroom. Another sip of tea warmed her through before she brushed her teeth.

"Can you see if Jessie is in her room," Julia called through the bathroom door, her toothbrush in her mouth. "Her alarm should have gone off by now."

Julia listened as Barker walked across the hallway and knocked on Jessie's door. There was no answer, and Julia did not hear movement in the room next door.

"She's not here," Barker called back. "Her bed hasn't been slept in."

Sighing, Julia spat out the toothpaste and wrapped her wet hair up in another towel. She rinsed her mouth and the brush, grabbed the empty cup, and walked back through to the kitchen.

"I don't know how I feel about her sleeping over at a boy's house," Julia said as she grabbed her phone off the kitchen counter. "Is seventeen too young?"

"I thought Billy and his dad were on holiday?" Barker mumbled as he walked out of the bedroom in his work suit. "Have I put too much wax in my hair?"

Julia shrugged as she pressed the phone against her ear. Her heart sunk to the pit of her stomach when it went straight to voicemail.

"She's either blocked my number, or Billy doesn't have a charger for her phone," Julia said as she lifted up a takeaway menu on the cork noticeboard. "Good job I went through her phone and wrote down her contacts."

"Isn't that an invasion of privacy?"

"No," Julia said quickly. "It's for emergencies."

"She's a teenage girl," Barker chuckled as he adjusted his hair, which Julia did think was too waxed, in the reflection of a knife. "Nobody forced her to storm out last night."

"Hmm," Julia said through pursed lips as she typed Billy's number into her phone. "I see a good night's sleep has made you believe you had no part in that."

"She *did* ruin the best chapter in my book," he muttered as he walked away. "I should set off. Chief wants us in for an early morning meeting. Unless it's to fill us in on the Astrid Wood case, I don't want to hear it."

Barker grabbed his briefcase, kissed Julia on the cheek, and headed for the door. Julia pushed the phone against her ear, relieved when she heard the dial tone.

"*W-what?*" Billy grumbled from the other end of the phone. "Who is it?"

"It's Julia," she said quickly. "Sorry if I woke you. I just wanted to check that Jessie was up for work. Her phone isn't turned on."

"Huh?"

"Can you just put Jessie on the phone?"

"Jessie's not here," he said, his voice clearing up.

"Has she already set off for work?"

"I'm still in Cornwall with my dad. Has something happened?"

Julia opened her mouth to reply, but all the moisture evaporated from her tongue.

"I'll call you back." Julia ended the call and hurried into the hallway, where Barker was tying his laces. "Barker, she's not at Billy's."

"What do you mean?" he asked, straightening out and rubbing his lower back. "Is there any reason your mattress is so hard?"

"I mean, she never went to Billy's last night,"

Fruit Cake and Fear

Julia said, her voice shaking as the towel on her head unravelled, letting down her damp hair. "She went out into that storm knowing Billy was still on holiday."

Julia thrust her hands up into her hair as the hallway walls closed in around her. Barker dropped his briefcase and planted his hands on her shoulder.

"Breathe," he said firmly. "Who else is on your list of numbers?"

Julia hurried back into the kitchen, clutching the towel around her chest as it began to slip. With shaky fingers, she ripped the list off the board and traced her finger down the handful of numbers.

"This is all she had."

"Okay, you start at the top, and I'll start at the bottom," Barker said, pulling his phone from his pocket. "She most likely left and then remembered Billy was on holiday."

Julia nodded, hoping he was right. She forced herself to focus on the first number, which was for her friend, Dolly.

"She's not here, Miss S," Dolly mumbled, still half asleep. "We haven't seen her since college on Wednesday."

Julia moved onto the next number, which was for Tommy, an elderly friend of Jessie's who had been a father figure to her on the streets. As she listened to the dial tone, a small part of her hoped Jessie was not with him because he now lived one hundred and seventy miles away in Manchester.

"I haven't seen her in months, Julia," Tommy said, the panic loud and clear in her voice. "Has something happened?"

Julia promised to call him back and quickly hung up.

"Nothing," Barker said, tossing his phone onto the counter. "Nobody has seen her."

"What have I done?" Julia mumbled, her eyes wide and her mind numb. "What if something has happened to her?"

"This is on me," Barker said, grabbing his keys from the counter. "What's the name of that place she used to hang around at when she was on the streets?"

"Fenton Industrial Park, but the last I heard they were turning it into luxury flats."

"It's worth a shot," he called over his shoulder as he headed to the front door. "It's somewhere familiar. Go and check the café. You never know, she might have just started work early."

The front door slammed, the letterbox rattling. Julia stared blankly at the list of names and numbers

Fruit Cake and Fear

for what felt like a lifetime before running into her bedroom. She jumped into the first clothes she could find, pulled her damp hair back into a bobble, and grabbed her keys. After locking the front door, she pulled out her car key, only to instantly remember it was still being fixed at the garage. Sighing, she ran around her cottage and grabbed her bike.

By the time Julia reached the village, her calves were starting to give way, and her face was wind burned, but she did not care. She fumbled with her keys until she landed on the one for her café. Just from looking through the window, she could see that Jessie was not there.

"Julia, love," she heard her gran cry. "I thought I saw you whizzing by on your bike. Oh dear, Julia, you know you haven't dried your hair, don't you?"

"Jessie is missing," Julia said, bursting into her café as Dot hurried across the village green. "She walked out last night, and I can't find her."

"Missing?" Dot cried, her hand drifting up to her mouth as she followed Julia inside. "Are you sure?"

"I – I don't know," Julia turned to face her gran and rested her hand against her forehead as she stared out of the window. "I don't know where she is."

"I'm sure she'll turn up," Dot said with a strained laugh. "Maybe she's at Billy's."

"Billy is on holiday," Julia snapped, pulling her phone from her pocket. "I'm calling the police."

"Okay, love," Dot said, pushing Julia into one of the seats. "You do that, and I'll make some tea."

Julia dialled '999' and reported Jessie missing. When she told the operator that Jessie was seventeen, she began to ask if it was possible that Jessie was with a friend, or if an argument had caused her to run away, making Julia feel even more to blame. The operator promised that an officer would come to see her soon to take Jessie's details before Julia hung up and tossed her phone onto the table. She planted her face in her hands, her mind whirring.

"Here you go," Dot said, resting a cup of peppermint and liquorice tea in front of her. "It's not like you to leave without cleaning up."

"What?"

"Your kitchen," Dot said, pushing up her curls as she sat across from Julia. "You've left it in a real state. Looks like a bomb's hit it. Flour *everywhere*."

Julia slid off her chair, knowing she had left the café spotless after closing the night before. She burst through the beads and into the kitchen. Somebody had been baking a cake on the stainless steel counter in the middle of the room, and just as Dot had mentioned, there was flour everywhere. Julia looked down at the flour covered floor, sure there were more footprints than one person could make.

"She was here," Julia called back. "Jessie was here."

"Does she always make such a mess?" Dot asked, following Julia into the kitchen. "Looks like she was having a food fight."

Julia walked around the edge of the room, not wanting to touch anything. Her initial relief at finding evidence of Jessie being in the café quickly vanished.

"If she was here, where is she now?" Julia thought aloud. "Look, these are her Doc Marten boot prints, but whose are these?"

"Maybe she had one of them twins in here with her?"

"I've already called them, and they haven't seen her since Wednesday," Julia mumbled, her bottom lip wobbling. "What if something has happened?"

Julia could not hold back the tears. Dot pulled her into a tight hug, rubbing the base of her neck, which was something she always did when Julia was a child.

"She'll walk through that door any minute," Dot said. "You watch. She's probably wandering around the village trying to clear her head as we speak."

At that very moment, the bell above the café door rang out, signalling the arrival of someone. Julia tore away from her gran before bursting through the beads, only to be disappointed to see Johnny wiping his feet on the doormat.

"Julia? Are you okay? You look –"

"Have you seen Jessie?" she asked as she hurried around the counter. "She's missing."

"Missing?" Johnny mumbled with a frown as he walked into the café, pulling his canvas messenger bag over his head. "Where has she gone?"

"I don't know, Johnny!" she cried, her cheeks burning red. "That's why she's missing!"

Johnny placed his bag on the chair Julia had been sitting in, fiddling with his glasses, before planting his hand on her shoulder. Julia could not hold back the tears and collapsed into his arms.

"Have you called the police?" Johnny asked as he patted her back awkwardly.

"They're on their way." Julia wiped her nose with the back of her hand as she pulled away from the hug she had forced upon her old friend. "Why are you here so early?"

Fruit Cake and Fear

"I was on my way to meet Sarah for a breakfast date at The Comfy Corner," he said, fiddling with his glasses as he blushed a little. "I saw your light and thought I'd drop in some photos I found in the archives at the office. I thought they might be useful. I couldn't see anything, but your mind works differently to everyone else's."

Johnny opened his bag and pulled out a thick frayed brown envelope. He pulled out a stack of photographs, but Julia's mind could not have been further from the Astrid Wood case if she tried.

"Johnny, I –"

"Your gran was right," he said as he flicked through the pictures. "Astrid really does look like Jessie."

Julia snatched the stack from him and flicked through, looking down at Astrid's face. Her heart sank as her mind pieced together a theory she did not want to accept.

"Julia?" Dot called tentatively from the kitchen. "I think you might want to see this."

Julia dumped the pictures and hurried through the beads. Her gran was holding a small piece of lined paper with a pair of metal tongs.

"I didn't want to touch it," she said. "I think you need to read this."

Julia took the tongs from her gran and looked down at the red writing on the scrap of lined paper, which looked like it had been hastily ripped from Julia's notepad.

"'*Help me, Julia,*'" she read aloud. "It's Jessie's handwriting."

"There's something on the other side," Dot said, gulping hard. "It looks like a circle."

Julia turned the paper over. There was a half-finished circle on the left side of the paper, but the red pen dribbled off the edge of the paper, as though her hand had been dragged away.

"Somebody has taken her," Julia said firmly, her eyes glazing over. "Whoever locked Astrid in the basement has taken Jessie."

"Why?" Dot asked, her brows pinching together. "What does Jessie have to do with this?"

"Absolutely nothing," Julia said, resting the tongs on the flour covered table. "But you said yourself how much Jessie looks like Astrid."

CHAPTER 13

"Hand these out!" Dot instructed, thrusting a fresh batch of missing posters in Shilpa's hands. "I want every person in this village to know Jessie's face. Amy, how are the search teams doing?"

"The ramblers are checking the Peridale trail," Amy said after checking the messages on her phone. "The Green Fingers are canvassing the rest of the village."

"Barker," Dot instructed, clicking her fingers to summon him across the café. "What's the latest on the door to door visits? Have your officers found anything yet?"

"Nothing yet, Dot," he called back, resting his phone against his shoulder. "I'm just talking to my boss now. They're rushing through the fingerprints they found in the kitchen. I've made sure to let them know it's urgent."

"Julia?" Dot said, hurrying through the full café. "How's the social media canvassing going?"

"People are sharing it all over the web," Julia said, resting her hand on her gran's shoulder. "A couple of people are saying they've seen similar girls, but nothing is confirmed yet. One guy asked me if she was wearing a yellow coat."

"That's definitely not Jessie," Dot said, checking her watch, and looking to the door. "Dolly and Dom should be back with the next batch of posters now. Those twins would be dangerous if they had a brain between them. What time are Billy and Jeffrey getting here?"

"In the next two hours," Julia said, checking the time on the laptop screen. "It's a four-hour ride from Cornwall. I don't know what they're going to do."

Fruit Cake and Fear

"Man power, my dear!" Dot exclaimed, leaving Julia's side, and hurrying to the door as Dolly and Dom hurried in with a fresh stack of posters from the printers at the library. "There you are! I was about to send out a search party for you two as well."

"We got lost," Dolly said.

"Couldn't remember where Julia's café was," Dom added.

"The library is around the corner!" Dot cried, taking the posters from them. "You better run back and print some more. The rambling club should be back soon, and I'm going to send them out to the surrounding villages."

The platinum-haired twins nodded enthusiastically and hurried out of the café. Barker finished his phone call and walked over. He kissed Julia on the top of the head before resting his hands on her shoulders.

"I've never seen your gran like this," Barker said. "She's running this whole thing."

"It might all be for nothing," Julia said, catching Barker's eyes in the reflection on the laptop. "What if –"

"Don't think like that." He squeezed her shoulders hard. "We're going to find her."

Julia pushed forward a smile, not wanting her

mind to go to the dark places it had been lingering on in the hours since discovering the note in her kitchen. The second the police had tried to dismiss her theory that the person who locked Astrid in the basement had also taken Jessie, Dot had jumped in and risen to the challenge in an instant. Nobody cared about a worthy cause like Dot.

"Where is Johnny?" Dot cried, checking her watch. "He was supposed to be back by now with the camera crew. We need blanket coverage. Somebody *will* have seen her!"

Julia looked up when the café door opened. She expected to see Johnny, so she was shocked when she saw Evelyn. The villagers in the café who had been calling everyone they knew to get them involved in the search were at once silenced by the appearance of the B&B owner.

"Oh, Julia!" Evelyn hurried across the café and wrapped her arms around her shoulders. "I've only just heard."

Julia closed her eyes and clung onto Evelyn. She buried her face in her kaftan, the scent of lavender and incense comforting her. If anyone knew how Julia was feeling, it was Evelyn.

"This is all strangely familiar," Evelyn said, glancing around the café uneasily as she pulled away from the hug. "Do you have any idea what has happened to her?"

Julia grabbed Evelyn's hand and led her out of the café to the alley. When the two women were alone, Julia's heart ached in her chest as she realised she was feeling a fraction of what the poor woman in front of her had been feeling for twenty years.

"Have you ever noticed how Jessie looks like Astrid?" Julia asked, glancing over her shoulder at the village green as the rambling group made their way towards the café. "Gran pointed it out, and I haven't been able to un-see it since."

"I did notice a certain similarity," Evelyn said, frowning a little. "Dark hair, pale skin. There are hundreds of girls out there who look like that. I can't tell you how many times I have seen teenage girls like that and thought they were Astrid. I had to remind myself she wouldn't be a teenage girl if she – *if* she had been alive."

Evelyn forced a smile, even though her eyes began to water. Even if it was only in a small way, she looked like she had accepted the fate of her daughter more than the last time Julia had seen her.

"You might think I'm crazy, but I think whoever locked Astrid in the basement took Jessie."

"I don't think you're crazy," Evelyn replied

bluntly. "If you believe something, I believe it too. But I need to ask, why do you think that?"

"Jessie was in the café last night. She left my cottage in the storm, and she came here." Julia paused, wishing once again she had tried harder to stop Jessie from leaving. "She was baking. It's something she has started to do when she needs to calm down. I think she learned it from me. She probably would have come home straight after, but I think someone came here and took her. She left a note to let me know she was in trouble, and she tried to leave me a message, but whoever took her stopped her."

"Do you know who took Astrid?" Evelyn asked, her fingers fumbling with the crystals around her neck.

"No."

"Do you know why they took her?"

"No." Julia looked down at the ground, embarrassed she had not figured it out. "I've been talking to everyone I can think of who might know what happened that night, but nobody seems to know anything that hasn't already been said."

"Or someone is lying."

"Most likely," Julia said with a firm nod. "But I don't know who. That's what I need to figure out. If

I do, I find Jessie and it —" Julia paused to choke back the tears. "– it might not be too late for her."

Evelyn's eyes rested on one of the crystals. She whispered something before kissing it. She pulled the thin rope over her head and placed the crystal around Julia's neck.

"Garnet," Evelyn said as she positioned the red stone in the centre of Julia's chest. "Astrid's birthstone. She has not come to me yet, but she might feel your pain and guide you to Jessie."

Before Julia could say anything, footsteps clicked on the cobbles behind her. She turned, hoping to see Jessie, but it was just Roxy.

"I couldn't leave school earlier," Roxy said as she ran towards Julia to hug her. "Hi, Evelyn. Oh, Julia! I've been worried sick all day. What can I do?"

"I don't know," Julia said as she clung to her best friend. "I can't lose her."

"You're not going to." Roxy pulled away and clutched Julia's hands. "I'm going to take my car and drive around. I might see something."

"Thank you," Julia said, not wanting to admit that if someone were going to see Jessie wandering around, they would have seen her already. "Maybe she's just out shopping or something and doesn't realise we're looking for her."

"That's what teenagers are like," Roxy said, brushing Julia's cheek with her thumb. "I'll call you if I see anything."

Roxy hugged Julia one last time before hurrying back down the alley towards her car. Julia turned back to Evelyn, who was smiling sadly at her.

"I was the same way in the beginning," she said. "I didn't want people to know how worried I was. A small part of me knew she was dead from the beginning, but this isn't what has happened here. I *feel* it, Julia. I *feel* Jessie's energy. I know you're not a believer, but believe me when I say I know she is going to turn up safe and well."

Evelyn and Julia clung to each other's hands for a moment, sharing a pain only they could understand. After Evelyn returned to her B&B, Julia walked back into her café, surprised to see Aiden and Grace talking to Barker. When Barker looked over their shoulders to smile at Julia, Aiden and Grace spun around.

"We can't believe it's happening again," Grace said, looking like she had been crying. "It doesn't make any sense."

"We came as soon as we heard," Aiden added as he tucked his scruffy blond hair behind his ears. "I've got the boys ringing all of their friends' parents to see if they've seen her. If there is anything we can do, we'll do it. We know what you're going through."

"You can hand some of these out," Dot said, thrusting a pile of posters into Aiden's chest. "Make yourself useful."

Aiden nodded and split the stack with Grace. They both looked over the picture of Jessie, their eyes lighting up at the same time.

"I've never seen her before," Aiden said. "She looks just like –"

"Astrid," Grace jumped in. "It's uncanny."

"There are plenty of girls out there with dark hair and pale skin," Dot exclaimed, pushing between them, and shoving them in the direction of the door. "Those posters aren't going to hand themselves out."

Grace and Aiden both smiled sympathetically over their shoulders at Julia as Dot forced them out of the door. When they were outside, Dot closed the door, turned, and rolled her eyes.

"I'm *still* not convinced he didn't kill her," she muttered through pursed lips. "I don't trust men with long hair."

"*Gran!*" Julia said. "Now isn't the time."

Dot shook her head and collapsed into one of the free chairs, clearly exhausted. She rubbed her temples before sipping her stone-cold cup of tea. Julia looked around the café, almost not believing that she had not offered anyone any cake yet. As she stood up to see what was in the fridge, Amy jumped out of her seat, her phone in her hand.

"Jessie always wears Doc Martens and a black hoody, doesn't she?" she asked, her eyes glued on her phone. "I've just had a picture message from Malcolm."

Amy walked forward, her hands shaking as she looked down at the phone. When she met Julia's eyes, Julia knew it was not good news.

"The Green Fingers have just found these in a river," Amy mumbled, turning the phone around. "I'm so sorry, Julia."

The floor disappeared from underneath Julia when she saw the grainy photograph of a soaked black hoody and shiny black Doc Martens on a riverbank. They were the same clothes Jessie had been wearing when she had left the cottage the night before. Without even realising it, Julia fell back into her chair.

CHAPTER 14

The seconds passed like days and the days like weeks. Julia could no longer distinguish between night and day, and only slept in small bursts when she could no longer keep her eyes open.

"I've made you some breakfast," Barker said as he walked into the dining room with a plate of toast. "Have you been up all night?"

"Is it morning?" Julia mumbled as she drummed her pen on the table, looking over the mountain of notes she had made. "What am I missing, Barker? I've mapped out everything I can find out leading up to Astrid's death, and I'm still nowhere near."

"It would be easier if Aiden *had* chopped her up and put her in the walls," he joked, forcing a smile before putting the toast on the edge of the table and stepping back. "Why don't you open the café today?"

"Because Jessie is still out there," she replied bluntly. "And it's my job to find her. Why didn't Astrid want to go to the prom? I thought she was in love with Aiden? What kept her away?"

"She was being bullied."

"But by who?" Julia asked. "And why the basement under the toy shop? Not a lot of people could have known it was there."

"Alistair has been interviewed half a dozen times, and he's sticking to the same story." Barker leaned against the doorframe, tilting his head to peer at some of Julia's scribbled notes. "'*Astrid knew about Grace's pregnancy*'."

"I think Astrid was the only person who knew until the baby came," Julia mumbled through a mouthful of toast. "I don't even think Doctor

Gambaccini knew about it."

"How can you hide a pregnancy from your mother?"

"Not everyone blows up like Sue," Julia said, grabbing at a picture of Grace at the prom with Aiden, which had been in the pictures Johnny had given to her. "She was wearing a floaty dress. According to Aiden, the baby grew under her ribcage, so she would have had a tiny bump."

"But what does that have to do with Astrid?"

"Well, nothing," Julia said, tossing the photo back. "But these two got married, and they're connected to Astrid. They were her only friends in a school full of people who thought her mother was weird."

"You don't think –"

"Don't."

"You don't know what I was going to say," Barker said softly with a small shrug. "I'm just *saying*. A lot of the time, it *is* the parents."

"Have you met Evelyn?" Julia asked with a roll of her eyes.

"Have you?" Barker snapped back with a forced laugh. "She *is* weird. You've seen her in a trance. She's a good actress."

"Not good enough to fake grief, Barker," Julia

said, cramming the last piece of toast into her mouth. "I looked into her eyes. I saw her pain."

"You saw what you wanted to see," he replied unsurely. "Or what she thought you wanted to see."

"Are you talking about the same person?" Julia could feel her voice starting to rise. "You're barking up the wrong tree as usual, Barker Brown."

"It would make a great twist for my book though."

"Are we forgetting Jessie is still missing?"

Barker's eyes suddenly darted to the floor, his smile dropping. Julia clenched her eyes shut, knowing she needed sleep, but also knowing the second she tried, her mind would start whirring in circles.

"What was Jessie trying to tell me?" Julia mumbled as she traced her finger over the half circle and squiggle she had recreated in red ink from memory. "What does this look like to you?"

"A worm going into a hole."

"Never mind."

Barker opened his mouth to speak, but their eyes locked when they heard a key rattling in the front door. Julia jumped up, the chair toppling over. She skidded into the hallway, her heart dropping when she saw her gran backing into the cottage as she shook off her umbrella.

"It's only me," she yelled as she turned to close the door. "Oh, a welcoming committee."

Julia pushed forward a smile to hide her obvious disappointment. Barker rested a hand on her shoulder and squeezed hard. She could not count how many times she had run into the hallway thinking Jessie was about to walk through the door like everyone kept reassuring her would happen.

"I thought I'd pop in and give you an update on the search," Dot said as she adjusted her hair in the hallway mirror. "And, to see if you've showered. I can see you haven't, but I think I might be able to smell it on my next visit, Julia."

"Any news?" she asked, not wanting to argue with her gran.

"Not yet," she said with an optimistic smile. "I've brought you some scones. They're shop bought, but I don't want you wasting away."

"I've eaten."

"More toast?" Dot asked, arching a brow as she pulled the scones from her handbag. "I thought so. You need to take better care of her, Barker."

Barker opened his mouth to defend himself, but Dot's icy stare silenced him, reducing him to give a feeble nod. Julia was grateful Barker had only been feeding her toast. She was not sure she could stomach anything else; not even her peppermint and liquorice tea could fix her.

Julia sat in the sitting room and forced down one of the scones as she stared out at the rain. Dot filled Julia in on the idle village gossip, and it seemed like Jessie had already dropped on their priority lists.

"And Amy Clark has been looking *everywhere* for that bucket," Dot said, wafting her hand. "It has brass handles too. I've told her it's a lost cause. I bet those thugs from Fern Moore have taken it."

Julia's phone beeped in her pocket. It was another text from Billy asking if there was any news. Julia replied and told him there was not anything yet, but there would be soon. She did not know who she was forcing the optimism for anymore.

"Is there anything else you can think of, Gran?" Julia asked. "Anything about that time that you haven't mentioned yet?"

"It was *twenty* years ago," Dot said with a sigh.

"And you can still tell me who won what at the 1948 Olympics," Julia replied quickly. "Anything."

"1948 *was* a good year. You know I would have been picked for the team if Ma hadn't held me back." Dot paused and finished her scone before turning and looking out of the window at the light rain. "It was a weird time. I remember seeing Evelyn everywhere, and then not at all. She turned into a recluse. Same as Aiden, but I don't think he dared show his face. Alessandra and that daughter of hers paraded the new baby, even if we all knew that Doctor Gambaccini was completely embarrassed that her perfect daughter was another teen pregnancy statistic. I don't think Grace had a choice but to become a doctor, if only to keep her mum onside. I can't imagine it was easy having a baby so young and keeping it a secret."

"What about the toy shop?"

"It was already closed by that point, if I'm remembering that right," Dot said, tapping the side of her head. "Alistair made a big song and dance about closing, and then it stayed empty for months. If it had crossed our minds that Astrid was down there, we would have dug that yard up in seconds."

"I know," Julia said. "I wouldn't have known if it wasn't for the storm. Maybe Jessie would still be here. I told her to leave the slab, but we lifted it anyway."

"She's too much like you," Dot said with a small smile. "Anyone would think she was your daughter by birth. You're so alike."

Julia tried to smile at the compliment, but it

took all her strength not to cry. She was proud to call Jessie her daughter, whether she gave birth to her or not, she just wished she had told her sooner.

***

AFTER FINALLY SHOWERING, JULIA loaded up on coffee and rode her bike into the village. She could not bring herself to look at her café, so she rode straight to the B&B, avoiding the missing posters covering every free surface.

"Julia," Evelyn said, smiling uneasily after opening the door. "What a pleasant surprise."

"Can I come in?" Julia asked, looking over Evelyn's shoulder. "Is it a good time?"

Evelyn glanced over her shoulder before nodding. She stepped aside and let Julia in. It was nice to see Evelyn wearing one of her familiar bright coloured kaftans and turbans, even if her eyes were still red raw.

"I was just trying to contact the other side," Evelyn explained as they walked into the candle filled room. "No luck so far. Astrid is still evading me."

"I'm sorry to hear that." Julia sat on the couch as Evelyn blew out the candles and turned on the lamps dotting the rooms. "I wanted to ask you something."

"Ask away."

Evelyn shuffled across the room and sat next to Julia. She gripped her hands, her eyes darting down to the crystal around Julia's neck. She had not taken it off, even to shower, since Evelyn had draped it around her neck.

"How did you do it?" Julia asked, her voice already shaking. "How did you do it day in and day out for so many years?"

Evelyn's smile faltered, her hands clenching Julia's.

"I *never* gave up hope," she whispered, leaning into Julia's face. "It was the only thing that got me out of bed in the morning. It didn't get easier over time. It felt like somebody cut off my arm and I never went to the hospital, and I just learned to live without it."

Julia wrapped her fingers around the crystal and closed her eyes. She begged the universe to give her a sign that Jessie was out there somewhere. She could not live for the next twenty years never knowing.

"I don't think I can do it. I'm not strong enough."

"Julia South, don't you *ever* say that," Evelyn

said sternly. "You have lived through the hardest things a person can experience, and you still serve people cakes with a smile. You lost your mother as a child, you came out of a divorce a stronger woman, and you've seen the worst humanity has to offer. I look up to you."

"You do?"

"Of course," Evelyn said. "Us women need to stick together. I'm here for you. I'm just down the road."

Julia nodded, understanding exactly what Evelyn was saying. As she looked into the woman's eyes, she felt like she was seeing the truest and most honest version of the B&B owner she had ever seen.

"Thank you, Evelyn," Julia said. "I think I needed to hear that."

"Humans are a beautiful contradiction. We're impossibly fragile, and yet stronger than we will ever realise. We have lived through wars, disasters, riots and storms, death and murder, and *some* of us have even lived through cults. It would be easy to give up and hold our hands up in defeat to the universe, but it is in the struggles that we learn who we are and what our purposes are. Even now, twenty years later, I still find myself in Astrid's bedroom once a week. You wouldn't think a scent would last that long, but

Fruit Cake and Fear

I can still smell her. Maybe it's in my imagination, but I don't suppose that matters, does it? It's when I feel closest to her. I think I may go in there soon. I haven't been able to face it since – *well*, since she was found dead. I can say that now. She deserves that ownership. Somebody locked my daughter in that basement, and they have to live with that until their day comes. I spent years blaming myself, but I can finally sleep with a clear conscience, and that's more than that animal can say."

Julia absorbed each of Evelyn's words and let them soak in. She had never given the B&B owner enough credit for her wisdom.

"Did you say you went in Astrid's bedroom?" Julia asked. "You still have it?"

"It's at the top of the house." Evelyn looked up at the ceiling with a small smile. "I could have turned it into another guest room. The Maker knows I needed the money for some years, but I couldn't bring myself to do it. It's become my temple. Untouched, aside from the police poking their noses around and taking things at will as evidence. I got things back eventually and put them exactly where Astrid had left them."

Julia looked up at the ceiling, wondering why she had never asked about Astrid's bedroom before.

It was exactly what Evelyn would do; turn her daughter's bedroom into her sanctuary.

"Can I see it?" Julia found herself asking before she thought about it.

"If that's what you want, of course you can. Forgive me if I don't follow you up. For all my talk of strength, I don't actually think I'm quite energised enough to face it today, but maybe tomorrow, or the day after. It's not going anywhere, is it? Follow the stairs up to the third floor. It's the door at the end of the hall. You can't miss it."

Julia left Evelyn in the dim sitting room and crept up the stairs, the building creaking underneath her. Julia walked around the first floor hallway and then up the second set of stairs and continued up the third until she reached her destination. Evelyn was right about not being able to miss the door at the end of the hall. From everything Julia knew about Astrid, it could only be her room.

Tiptoeing as softly as she could, Julia approached the oak door, which had been decorated in silver and gold marker pen stars and crescent moons. A dream catcher hung from a nail in the centre of the door, a sprig of dried sage hanging from one of the beads.

Julia reached out for the doorknob, unsure of

what she hoped to find. Anything of significance was likely sitting in a box in the police station across the road, but Julia felt the sudden urge to feel as close to Astrid as she could. She shared more than a face with Jessie; she also shared a free spirit and the status of a misunderstood outsider.

Holding her breath, Julia opened the door and slipped into the room. The small room was dark and musty, not unlike Jessie's. It had started raining and the sound of it beat down on the exposed wooden roof, soothing Julia. She closed the door behind her and flicked on the light. The pink paper lampshade above her sent a warm wash across the small space. The walls were covered in posters from David Bowie's youth, which was before Astrid's time, as it was Julia's. The surfaces were filled with crystals and candles, and other trinkets from around the world, proving that she was Evelyn's daughter to the core.

Leaning over a chest of drawers, Julia peeled back the curtain and peered through the circle window, which looked down at the street below. She watched as Barker pulled up outside the station, talking quickly into his phone as he pushed on the door and disappeared inside.

Julia let the curtain fall and looked down at the pictures on the desk, not wanting to touch anything.

She poured over the various photographs of Astrid and Evelyn, which were scattered amongst pictures of Astrid and Aiden, looking every inch the loved up teenage couple. Something pure radiated through the pictures, telling Julia it was much more than the school flings she had seen and experienced herself.

She walked over to the dressing table, which looked like it had also been used as a desk. Dust-covered bottles of perfume and lotions cluttered the surface, along with fluffy gel pens in every pastel shade imaginable, and a stack of cassette tapes from bands Julia vaguely remembered from her own school days.

There was a scrapbook in the centre, one page red, and the other black. The double-page spread Astrid had been working on was titled '*The Final Days of Normal*'. It featured a picture of Astrid along with the rest of her class in the classic Hollins High School green and black blazer Julia remembered. Beneath it were three pictures of Astrid and Aiden, all of which Julia had copies of at home thanks to Johnny. On the black side, there was a single picture featuring Astrid, Aiden, and Grace at the lakes. It was similar to the picture Julia had seen in their yearbook but from a different angle. Where the other had been from the front on, this one had been taken from the side, and Julia could even see the person taking the version of the picture she had seen.

Julia brushed her fingers against the picture, and it moved under her touch. She carefully slid it off the page and lifted it up to her face. Astrid was wearing heavy black clothes, which jumped out against Aiden's swimming shorts and Grace's frilly bikini. Grace's blonde hair shone under the bright sun, as though it was naturally that colour. She was still a slender woman, but her teenage frame was something Julia had never experienced herself at that age. Her stomach was completely flat, almost convex, and her ribs shone under her bikini top. Julia turned the photograph over. It had been dated '*June 27th, 1997 – Lake District*' in glittery pink ink. Julia turned the picture around again, and frowned before flipping it back again. She wondered if there had been a mistake, but she remembered the school trip herself two years before in 1995, and it had been in June to celebrate the end of their final exams.

Julia placed the photo where she had found it. She stepped back before turning, the edge of her shoe catching on the woven rug covering the dusty floorboards. She put her hands out to catch herself and fell into the wall. There was an almighty rip as her hand planted through David Bowie's lightning bolt covered face on the poster next to the door.

Clutching her hand, Julia looked at the ground, hoping Evelyn had not heard her tumble. She looked at the poster, wondering if there was a way to fix it. Bowie frowned back at her, his nose and mouth curling into the wall. Julia fingered the edge of the ripped paper and pulled it back to see what was behind it. Her stomach fluttered when she saw a hollow space behind the poster. Julia glanced over her shoulder at the picture on the desk, hoping Astrid would forgive her for invading her privacy. Julia wondered how many police searches the hole behind the poster had survived. It reminded her of the loose floorboard in her bedroom at her gran's, where she had hidden the Jilly Cooper novels she had bought at the charity shop with her pocket money.

Teasing carefully on the twenty-year-old sticky tack, Julia pulled the poster away from the top and let it hang down. The hole covered most of the surface of the paper, and looked like it had been created by a hammer, and then made bigger by ripping at the edges. Within the space between the frame and the plaster board there was a rusty old bent nail, and on that nail hung a dust covered crushed velvet satchel. Holding her breath, Julia reached in and pulled the bag off the hook, no doubt for the first time in twenty years.

Julia pulled on the frayed gold thread and dust flew everywhere. She peered into the bag and was met with a plastic white lid. She reached inside and pulled out the bottle, along with a piece of cardboard, which fluttered to the ground. Julia turned the bottle over in her hands, recognising them as a brand of pre-natal vitamins, similar to ones her sister was taking for the twins. The prescription label was faded, but Julia could just make '*Grace Gambaccini*' by squinting and holding it up to the pink light.

Julia bent over and picked up the cardboard, which had moulded to the shape of the bottle. Turning it over, she stared at the warped grainy pregnancy scan picture, the tiny baby reminding her of the one of Sue's twins stuck to her fridge. Julia turned it over, Grace's name also on this. She looked back at the photograph on the desk and pulled out her phone. She took pictures of the bottle and the scan, along with both sides of the photograph.

When she was finished, Julia stepped back, her heart stopping dead in her chest. The penny finally dropped, and she knew who had locked Astrid in the basement, and more importantly, why.

Agatha Frost

CHAPTER 15

After getting their address from Roxy, Julia stared at the picture by the lake on her phone for the whole taxi journey to Aiden and Grace's house in Burford. She only looked up when they passed The Flying Horseman.

"That's sixteen quid, darlin'," the taxi driver said, tapping his finger on the red LED meter on the dashboard.

Julia thrust a twenty-pound note into his hand and told him to keep the change. She looked at the small detached cottage and checked the address Roxy had texted her to make sure she had the right place. Aiden and Grace lived in a nice white cottage with a classic thatched roof on the corner of a bending street. They had a small, well-tended garden and beautiful curtains in the window. Despite the grey sky above, the old cottage was everything one would expect to find in the Cotswolds.

Not wanting to waste any time, Julia unclipped the gate and hurried down the winding path to the black front door. She knocked firmly three times before looking down at her phone screen, which had faded to black, reflecting back her image. Her dishevelled appearance took her by surprise, the purple bags under her eyes so heavy she considered charging them rent. Her usual chocolatey curls were scraped back into a bobble, still damp from her shower. Julia rarely wore makeup, but her fresh complexion was sallow and grey from the lack of sleep and a diet of toast and butter for how ever many days it had been since Jessie went missing. Was it four, or six? She shook her head, her brain unable to focus.

The door opened, but instead of Aiden and

Fruit Cake and Fear

Grace, it was Mark, their eldest son. His jet-black hair was straightened over his eyes, almost covering them. Smoky eyeliner lined his eyes, and there was a black studded choker around his neck. The scratchy blur of an electric guitar drifted out from deep within the house.

"Can I help you?" he mumbled, looking down at Julia as she stared at him, unable to do anything else.

"Do you remember me?" she asked, smiling weakly. "We met at the pub the other night. Your dad's gig?"

"Oh, yeah," Mark mumbled as he squinted at Julia, his confusion and disinterest loud and clear. "Are you the one who –"

"She's called Jessie," Julia said quickly. "Are your parents home?"

"My dad's in the back practising," Mark said, hooking his thumb over his shoulder. "We've got a gig at The Railway tonight."

"It won't take long," Julia said, shuffling past Mark and into the cottage, feeling like her gran all of a sudden. "You're into David Bowie, aren't you?"

"Yeah," Mark said, arching his dark brows over his heavy makeup lined eyes as he closed the door. "How do you know?"

"Your mum mentioned it," Julia said quickly.

"Remember? At the pub?"

"Oh, yeah," he mumbled again. "Are you okay? You're a little – *twitchy*."

Julia quickly realised she was blinking more than usual. When had she last slept? The fact she could not remember did not bode well. She straightened up and tried to tell her face to play along, but it was getting harder and harder to fight off the sleep deprivation shaking her brain.

"Just a little tired," Julia said, smiling wide. "Your dad's in the back, did you say?"

Before Mark could answer, Julia hurried through the cottage, following the sound of the electric guitar. Aiden was in the conservatory, one foot on a speaker as his fingers danced over the strings, his blond hair hanging low over his face. Julia cleared her throat, but he was so deep into the song she did not recognise, she went unnoticed.

"*Dad!*" Mark called over the noise before pulling the plug on his guitar. "Guest."

Aiden looked up and swished his hair away from his face, and for a moment, he looked just like the boy by the lake on the picture on her phone. Just as good looking then as he was now, albeit with more fine lines and pock marks.

"Julia?" Aiden cried, displaying a similar

confused look as his son. "What a surprise. I didn't know you knew where we lived. How are you holding up?"

"Not great," Julia said, glancing at the speaker. "I hear you have a gig tonight?"

"I usually practice in the attic. It's soundproofed for the sake of the neighbours, but I can't for the life of me find the key." He pulled the guitar over his head and rested it against a wicker chair. He offered Julia a seat, but she felt better standing. "If you're looking for Grace, she's gone to pick up her mother. Thursday is the in-law dinner night. I'd rather do without it, but what can you do?"

"It's Thursday?" Julia mumbled.

"I remember what it feels like for the days to blur into one," Aiden said, smiling under his hair at her, his eyes surprisingly dark against his blond hair. "Can I get you something? Something to eat, or a drink?"

"No," Julia said, her mind racing. Why was she there? She blinked hard and forced her mind to focus. "Your relationship with Astrid. Was it – were you –"

Before Julia could think of what she wanted to say, the front door opened and Alessandra's voice floated through to the conservatory.

"I've told you *repeatedly*, nothing good comes from living near a main road, Grace!" Julia heard her say. "You get all of the vagrants and runts of society walking past your door. You need some net curtains up in those windows. Any old drunk can look in."

They both walked past the conservatory door with plastic shopping bags, neither of them looking in Julia's direction. Mark walked past, catching her gaze. He looked unsettled by her presence.

"What was it you said you wanted?" Aiden said, scratching the side of his head.

"I didn't," Julia mumbled. "I –"

"*Julia!*" Grace cried, stopping in her tracks as she walked into the conservatory. "What a surprise!"

Alessandra followed her daughter in, her eyes narrowing when she spotted Julia.

"She's the one I told you about," the former doctor whispered indiscreetly.

"Julia was just about to tell me why she is here," Aiden said, folding his arms across his chest. "Weren't you?"

She could tell he was growing increasingly irritated by her unexpected visit. Julia blinked hard, glancing up at the ceiling. She remembered everything she had seen in Astrid's bedroom, her thoughts gathering into one place long enough for her to focus on the words.

"Do you know that you're Mark's father?" Julia asked, looking Aiden dead in the eyes.

"What sort of question is that?" he replied, forcing a laugh. "Of course I'm his father. I've raised him since birth."

"I meant to say biological father," Julia continued. "You're Mark's *biological* father."

"What?" Aiden muttered, laughing even more. "I think you should go home and get some sleep, Julia. Things have been tough for you recently, so I'll let it slide this time."

"Tell him, Grace," Julia said, turning to the doctor. "Tell him how you stole Astrid's baby."

Grace's mouth dropped as she looked from her husband to the stranger in her house. Julia was so focussed on waiting for what Grace had to say, she did not notice Alessandra picking up the lamp until it was too late.

"You should have kept your nose out of where it wasn't wanted, you stupid girl."

The heavy lamp hit the back of Julia's head, smashing on contact. She collapsed into a heap on the floor, her lids clamping shut. It was impossible to resist slipping into the darkness.

***

JULIA WAS NOT SURE HOW LONG SHE had been unconscious for, but she knew she was no longer in the conservatory. She was sitting up in a wooden chair, but she could not move. She forced her eyes open and looked down at the fabric tying her arms and legs to the chair, a similar fabric gagging her mouth.

"I've kept this a secret for twenty years," she heard a deep voice growl. "Twenty *bloody* years, and now *this*."

Julia squinted into the dark and watched as Alessandra paced back and forth, a shiny kitchen knife in her hand. Grace was leaning against a red chimneybreast, rocking and hitting her head against the brick as she mumbled under her breath, her eyes wide and distant. Her pupils suddenly flicked up, connecting with Julia's.

"Mother. She's awake."

Alessandra stopped pacing and looked at Julia, the knife primed. Julia moaned behind the gag, unsure of if she was trying to beg for her life or scream for help. She heard a similar noise come from her side. She turned her head, the collision from earlier blurring her vision as she realised the back of her head was bleeding. Julia let out a deep moan when she saw Jessie in the chair next to her. Tears tumbled down both their cheeks when their eyes locked.

"There's no point struggling," Alessandra said with a small laugh. "I was a doctor. I know how to knot a bandage properly."

Despite the warning, Julia thrashed against the chair, her eyes fixed on Jessie. She was wearing a pair of bright pink pyjamas, which clashed with her icy skin that was paler than usual. Julia looked around the room she was in, realising it was the attic. She tried to scream out for help, immediately remembering what Aiden had said about it being soundproofed.

"I told you she was back, Mother," Grace mumbled, pointing a shaky finger at Jessie. "I *told* you."

"When did you take your last pill?"

"I don't *need* them." Grace dropped her head like a naughty child. "I think better *without* them."

Alessandra sighed and scratched at her head with the handle of the knife. She turned to her daughter, rolled her eyes, and then turned back to Julia.

"None of this would have happened if you had just left the girl where she was," she snapped through thin lips. "What has it achieved? You got yourself into this mess."

Julia forced her tongue against the bandage in her mouth, and it rolled down her bottom lip and onto her chin. Julia took in a deep breath, turning to Jessie, trying to convey a message of strength through her eyes.

"Let Jessie go," Julia said. "She's done nothing."

"It's *her*!" Grace cried, her voice bouncing off the insulated walls. "*She's* come to take him."

"*She* is dead!" Alessandra snapped over her shoulder. "Will you just shut up? You've already made this worse."

Grace retreated back into herself and nodded at her mother. Alessandra began to pace again, the knife by her side.

"I know what happened," Julia said. "I know you weren't pregnant, Grace. Not with Mark at least."

"You don't know *anything*!" Alessandra snapped. "Nobody is going to give you a gold star for figuring it out."

"I know your daughter was in love with Aiden," Julia flicked her eyes to Alessandra's. "I know she was the one bullying Astrid at school. Everyone thought it was odd that Grace and Aiden got together so soon after Astrid disappeared, but that was the plan all along, wasn't it, Grace? You were so in love with your best friend's boyfriend that you couldn't bear to see her have his baby."

"That *stupid* girl was just like her mother," Alessandra hissed, pointing the knife at Julia. "Evelyn was only a child when she got pregnant too. It must run in the family. We were doing her a favour."

"By taking her to the hospital appointments and pretending she was your daughter?" Julia jumped in. "I found the scan and the pre-natal vitamins in Grace's name."

"They would have wanted to speak to her mother," Alessandra said. "She was only sixteen. A *child!* Children should not do adult things if they cannot handle the consequences. We were never going to take the baby. That was *never* the plan. The girl was dead regardless."

Julia did not respond. She had not had time to think this part of the story through, so she listened, encouraging Alessandra to talk with a shaky nod. Alessandra pursed her lips, glanced back at her daughter, and then snapped back on Julia like a sniper.

"It was the day of prom," she said, her voice

softening a little, but her gaze icy. "Astrid couldn't fit into her dress. We tried our best to find her something floaty. The child was barely showing, but she was scared everyone would see. She told Aiden she wasn't going and she called Grace. Grace wasn't a bully, she just had – *issues*. She had a crush on Aiden, and she took it out on Astrid. The girl knew she didn't mean it. They always made up."

"She tried to flush her head down the toilet." Julia could not help but jump in. "And probably while she was pregnant too."

Alessandra glanced at her daughter again as she rhythmically hit her head into the red brick.

"As I said, she was *troubled*," she continued. "Astrid called Grace on the day of the prom and told her that her stomach hurt. I knew her contractions had started. It was early, but it often is with girls of her age. Her contractions were so close together, she wouldn't have made it to the hospital where we'd arranged her birthing plan. She insisted she didn't want to go to the local general. Her mum had friends there, and she didn't want her to know. We'd already arranged the adoption. It was going to be seamless. I had to think fast –"

"So, you took her to Alistair's workshop," Julia said. "The basement under my café. I suspect you knew about it because of the affair you were having."

"How did you know about that?" Alessandra asked with a bitter laugh. "That was *decades* ago."

"You treated him like rubbish at the nursing home, and he let you," Julia said. "That's unrequited love if ever I've seen it."

"I told the old fool to stay with his wife. He only moved to the nursing home because I was there. We used to meet in the workshop, after hours, but it was never serious." Alessandra paused and shook her head as though realising she was getting off subject. "We took her down into the workshop. It all happened so fast. I wasn't a midwife. I hadn't delivered any babies since my training days. I was a GP. The baby was there, crying in Grace's arms within minutes. Astrid lost a lot of blood. We couldn't save her."

"You could have given her the dignity she deserved," Julia muttered through clenched teeth. "But instead, you ripped her baby away from her, and left her down there, all alone. And then Grace went to the prom and pretended like nothing had happened."

"She was *dead*!" Alessandra cried. "We didn't kill her! Why would we want to do that? I couldn't report it. They would have found out I was pretending she was my daughter and arranging an adoption. I would have been struck off the medical register! I wanted to go through with the adoption but –"

"Grace had other ideas," Julia said.

"She fell in love with Mark instantly," Alessandra said, her eyes dropping to the floor. "They bonded like they were really mother and son, in a way even I didn't with my own daughter. I couldn't rip him away from another mother, so I allowed it."

"And lied to everyone, acting like you didn't know and that you were outraged about your daughter having a teenage pregnancy." Julia paused, blinking hard as she felt the blood trickle down the back of her head. "I bet that was difficult for you. Swallowing your pride to cover up your lies. How did you get Alistair to pave up the yard and hide any existence of the basement?"

Alessandra gulped, blinking hard before glancing back at her daughter.

"I told him Aiden murdered her," Alessandra said, clearly not wanting Grace to hear. "I knew he would do anything to protect his nephew. He never had children, and he always looked at Aiden like he was his own son."

Fruit Cake and Fear

"That's sick," Julia mumbled, gulping through her dry mouth. "Even for you, that's sick."

"It was *necessary!*" she cried, lifting up the knife again. "At least the baby was raised by his *real* father!"

"Another necessary lie?"

"Aiden didn't even know Astrid was pregnant. It was no mistake that they bonded so quickly. It was like the baby knew who he was. It's only recently that Mark has started to question his father's authority. I suppose it was bound to happen. If Grace is anything to go by, those years can be somewhat – *difficult.*"

"And in all of this, did you think about Evelyn?" Julia asked, her vision beginning to blur. "The real victim here. She spent twenty years hoping her missing daughter would reappear, all the while the grandson she never knew existed was living thirty minutes down the road. How do you think she's going to feel when she finds out?"

"Finds out?" Alessandra laughed. "What do you mean? She's not going to *find out*. Aiden and Mark will take some convincing, but you two are going to be easy to deal with. I'd rather it was just you, but my daughter had to bring this one home last week. She came to find you to see what you knew after I told her you were sniffing around and asking questions, but she saw Jessie and had one of her *episodes*. Convinced herself this girl is Astrid's reincarnation. I must admit, the similarities are striking."

"It wasn't a half-finished circle," Julia whispered, turning to Jessie, who looked like she was fading in and out of consciousness. "It was the beginning of a '*G*'. You were trying to write '*Grace*'."

A distant thud shuddered through the floor. Was it thundering again? Julia listened out for rain until she remembered the soundproofing.

"I'm sorry, but I can't let either of you leave here," Alessandra said, running the knife along her finger. "You understand why, don't you? I've spent twenty years keeping this secret, and I made a promise to myself that I would take it to the grave, and that's what I'm going to do."

"She's *back*," Grace mumbled, the thud happening again. "She's *here*. She's *back*!"

Julia suddenly felt the crystal around her neck. Was it burning against her skin, or was the pain from her head spreading?

"She's *here*," Grace cried, clamping her hands over her ears. "She's come to take *my* baby away."

The thudding grew louder and louder.

Fruit Cake and Fear

Alessandra looked around, the knife glittering in the dim light. Julia turned to Jessie, whose head was rolling around on her shoulders.

"*Stay awake, love,*" Julia whispered. "*For me.*"

Jessie forced her eyes open and nodded. She attempted to smile through the gag.

"Astrid is *here*," Grace cried, her voice growing with the thudding. "She's *finally* come back. I *knew* this day would come!"

"Be *quiet!*" Alessandra cried. "I'm going to finish this once and for all."

Alessandra turned to Julia, the knife high in the air. The two women locked eyes, and Julia tried to convey her maternal pain to the mother in front of her, hoping she would understand. There was a flicker of recognition for a brief moment, but it vanished as quickly as it had arrived. Alessandra gritted her jaw and lifted the knife higher above her head, ready to strike.

Julia mentally apologised to Jessie for failing her. She tried to visualise her mother waiting for her on the other side, but the pain in the back of her head was so hot, she could not remember her face.

"*No!*" she heard Jessie cry out.

Julia opened her eyes, but everything happened too fast for her to stop it. Jessie rocked on her chair, thrusting herself in front of the blade. It struck her shoulder, leaving Alessandra's grip as Jessie fell to the ground. The chair shattered into pieces, freeing her as she lay on her back, the knife sticking straight up from her prone body.

"*Jessie!*" Julia cried out, her voice hoarse. "What did you do?"

There was one final thud before a trap door inches from Jessie's head burst open. Light flooded the attic, followed by glowing white hair. Julia squinted, wondering if Astrid really had come from the other side to save them.

"Grace?" Aiden cried as he climbed into the attic. "What is —"

"Call an ambulance!" Julia cried as Aiden's eyes landed on the knife jutting out of Jessie's motionless body. "Please, Aiden. Just like Mark is your child, Jessie is mine."

"Who did this?" he asked, his face disappearing into his blond hair.

"*She* did!" Alessandra cried, pointing at her daughter. "She's gone *mad!* She's *always* been mad! She *kidnapped* this girl and *stabbed* her!"

Grace continued rocking and mumbling to herself, not acknowledging her mother.

"Alessandra stabbed her," Julia cried.

Fruit Cake and Fear

"Ambulance, Aiden!"

Aiden and Alessandra stared at each other for a moment before she attempted to run for the opening in the floor. Aiden jumped in the way and rugby tackled the nimble woman to the ground. Julia tugged her hands, but the bandages were knotted impossibly tight. A mass of black hair popped up through the trap door, a phone to his ear.

"Ambulance, please," Mark said. "And police. That missing girl, Jessie, is here, and she's been stabbed. Hurry."

Julia smiled her gratefulness at the boy, who the more she looked at, the more she saw Evelyn. She looked over at Alessandra and Aiden as they struggled against each other on the ground. Julia considered asking Grace to untie her, but she did not want to risk disturbing her. Closing her eyes, Julia rocked back and smashed the chair against the floorboards. To her relief, the chair shattered, enabling her to wriggle free from her restraints.

"I'm here," Julia whispered, clutching Jessie's hand. "You're going to be okay. Just try and stay awake."

Jessie's eyes fluttered, connecting with Julia's momentarily. She opened her mouth to try and speak, but Julia shushed her, not wanting her to waste her energy.

"*Mum*," Jessie croaked, before slipping into unconsciousness.

CHAPTER 16

J ulia had never seen such a well-attended funeral in all of her years in Peridale. Hundreds of people crowded outside St. Peter's Church as Evelyn led the parade towards the church. Behind her, Astrid's coffin floated on the shoulders of half a dozen men, two of them being Aiden and Mark.

Barker wrapped his fingers around Julia's and squeezed.

Instead of flowers, the shiny black coffin was topped with hundreds of multi-coloured crystals, each of them shining delicately in the bright sun, which was poking through the milky clouds. It had been raining continuously in the week since Grace, Alessandra, and Alistair's arrests, but today was the first day Julia had seen the sun.

Evelyn caught Julia's eyes, and the two women shared a look only they understood. Julia nodded, and Evelyn nodded right back.

The service was a lengthy one, but it did not feel dragged out. Evelyn opened the eulogies with a heart-felt speech about her daughter's life, which followed by a speech from Aiden, which was noticeably absent of references to his wife. Julia shed her fair share of tears. Some of them were for Astrid's stolen life, others were for the time lost between Mark and Evelyn, and the rest were from sheer relief that everything was over.

After the service, the village flooded out of the church, all milling around the edge of the village green. Evelyn made her way through the crowd, which parted like the Red Sea, her rainbow kaftan fluttering delicately in the wind.

Fruit Cake and Fear

"You have given me the best gift I could have ever asked for," Evelyn beamed, taking Julia's hands in hers. "Not only have you given me closure and allowed my daughter to finally rest, you've given me a piece of her back."

Evelyn looked over her shoulder as Mark and Aiden talked to a group of other men. Mark looked up and smiled at his grandmother.

"I'm sorry you missed so much time," Julia said.

"Today is not a day for the word '*sorry*'!" Evelyn exclaimed, clapping her hands together. "Today is to celebrate my daughter's life and her new legacy in her son. I can feel her love surrounding him, and I suspect she's been there with him his whole life. I'm sure she'll connect with me now that she had been laid to rest. I must go to The Plough and put some of that Peridale Green Fingers' prize money that I won last month behind the bar. It's time to party!"

Evelyn scurried across the village green, her kaftan wafting dramatically behind her, reminding Julia of the time she had watched *Joseph and the Amazing Technicolor Dreamcoat* in the West End.

"Did we miss it?" Dot cried as she scurried along the street panting for breath, Jessie right by her side with her arm in a sling. "Don't tell me we missed it!"

"It was beautiful," Julia said, looping her fingers

around Jessie's free arm. "How are you feeling?"

"All the better for having my dressing changed." Jessie nodded at her shoulder. "Doctor said I'm going to have a pretty cool scar, but I think my driving test will have to wait for a while."

"Kids these days," Dot said, rolling her eyes. "Millimetres away from severing an artery and you think a scar is *cool!* I wonder if Evelyn is putting on a good buffet spread at the pub."

Following her stomach, Dot headed in the direction of The Plough with some of the other guests. Julia pulled Jessie to the side and waited for Aiden and Mark to make their way over. When they finally did, both men shared the same sheepish smile, neither of them quite able to look at Julia or Jessie.

"I suppose I should thank you," Aiden said as he tucked his scruffy hair behind his ears. "You've given me answers to questions I've been plagued with for most of my life."

"I've torn your family apart," Julia said.

"No, *she* did that," Aiden snapped. "You've brought my real family closer together. Mark, Evelyn, and my other two sons are my true family. I never stopped loving Astrid. There wasn't a day – you don't want to hear any more of this. I just wanted to make sure you knew that I don't blame you, and that I'm sorry for what they put you both through. I always knew Alessandra was an evil witch, but seeing her throw her daughter under the bus like that only confirmed it. I hope they throw the book at her."

"And your uncle?"

"He was lied to as much as anyone," Aiden said, sucking the air through his teeth. "I'm hopeful the jury will see that. He thought he was protecting me. I just hate that he's been thinking that about me for twenty years. It doesn't make him any different than the rest of the village, but you don't expect that from your own family, do you? I can't blame him now. He's an old man, I just hope he won't spend the years he has left rotting in a prison cell. Mark and I are lucky we're not being prosecuted too. We helped Alessandra get you up into the attic, and for that, we're both truly sorry, aren't we, Mark?"

"Yeah," he grumbled, glancing at them from under his black fringe. "It was mad."

"She told us you killed Astrid and she wanted to keep you there so she could call the police," Aiden continued. "I was so confused. We both were. We didn't understand what was happening. If I had known Jessie was up there too, I would never have gone through with it, but it was dark. I didn't see her. She said you were dangerous. She used the words '*mentally imbalanced*'. Ironic, right? The second we realised it didn't feel right, we beat that door through with a sledgehammer. I can't believe how stupid I was. I should have seen right through it, not just now, but two decades ago."

"Regardless of what happened, you still had twenty years of those people in your lives," Julia said, making sure to look both men in the eyes. "It couldn't have been all bad."

"I'm sure in time, I might see it that way." Aiden shrugged and stuffed his hands in his trouser pockets. "Grace's lawyers are going for an insanity plea, and quite frankly, I think she might get it. I knew she had problems, but she never told me how bad. I just thought it was a bit of depression, and that's why she took the pills. She always went a little funny when she drank with them, but nothing like what I saw in that attic. I always suspected she dyed her hair black to look like Astrid, but I didn't want to think she'd do something so sick."

"You should get to the pub," Julia said, nudging Mark's arm. "You have a lot to learn about your grandmother. She's a pretty cool lady. You have her eyes."

Fruit Cake and Fear

"They're Astrid's eyes too," Aiden said, looking at his son. "I feel like a fool for not seeing it before."

Aiden rested his hand on his son's shoulder, and they joined the stragglers walking towards The Plough. Jessie went to follow them, but Julia pulled her back and waited until they were standing outside the church alone. They both sat on the low stone wall and stared out at the village green as it emptied. Julia's eyes wandered over to the front of her shiny fixed car, which was poking out from its usual spot in the alley next to her café.

"I've been wanting to mention this since it happened, but I didn't know how to bring it up," Julia started, gripping Jessie's hand in hers. "You might not remember, but when Alessandra stabbed you, you said something. You called me '*Mum*'."

"I didn't mean to," Jessie mumbled, her cheeks blushing. "It just slipped out."

"I want to adopt you, Jessie," Julia said firmly, looking her dead in the eyes. "We've been through a lot this year, a lot of bad, but also a lot of good. As far as I'm concerned, you are my daughter, but I want to make it official before you turn eighteen next year."

Jessie opened her mouth to speak, but she appeared to not know what to say. Julia wondered if she had made a terrible mistake, but she had not been able to stop thinking about it since waking up in the hospital the morning after their ordeal.

Just when Julia thought Jessie was about to reject her offer, Jessie wrapped her single arm around Julia's neck and squeezed harder than she had before.

"What do I call you?" Jessie asked.

"Mum, Julia, '*Cake Lady*'," Julia said. "It doesn't make a difference to me. It doesn't change how I feel. I can't imagine what you went through in those days in that attic, but I went through hell on Earth without you. As a wise woman once said to me, I felt like I'd had my arm chopped off and I hadn't gone to the hospital to have it fixed."

"Is that supposed to be funny?" Jessie mumbled, nodding at her shoulder.

Julia winked and nudged Jessie. Hand in hand, they walked towards The Plough and joined the rest of the village. Barker was waiting for them at a table in the corner. He waved when he saw them. Jessie's boyfriend, Billy, was standing by the bar with his father, Jeffrey, no doubt trying to convince him to buy him a beer. Jessie slipped away from Julia, grabbed Billy, and kissed him.

"Looks like you asked her," Barker said as Julia sat next to him. "And she said yes, I presume?"

"She did," Julia said, looping her fingers around Barker's. "You never know. She might say yes to what you suggested to me if you asked her."

"It's too soon," Barker whispered with a half-smile. "Adoption is a long process. I don't want to freak her out, but in those days when she was gone, I felt like I'd –"

"Had your arm chopped off?"

"How did you know?" Barker said, squinting at her. "You're a witch, Julia South. We argue like cat and dog, but I love the kid like I raised her. It's impossible not to."

"I love that you love her," Julia replied, kissing Barker on the cheek. "And I love you. If you are serious about adopting her too, you'll ask her when the time is right."

Jessie walked over hand-in-hand with Billy, with Jeffrey, Dot, and Sue trailing behind all carrying two drinks each.

"Did you ask him yet?" Jessie asked, letting go of Billy's hand and squishing between Julia and Barker.

"I was waiting for you to get back," Julia said, budging over to make room.

"Ask me what?" Barker replied with an unsure smile as he looked around the group. Dot and Sue both shrugged, but Jessie gave them a knowing smile. "Spit it out!"

"We'd like to invite you to live with us," Jessie

said, wrapping her one arm around Barker's shoulder. "On a permanent basis, but there's one condition!"

"I become your servant?" Barker said, ruffling Jessie's hair. "Fat chance!"

"That's a good idea, but no," she said, dodging out of the way, and tucking her bushy hair behind her ears. "You stop leaving your underwear next to the washing basket, and you start –"

"Putting it in the basket?" Sue jumped in. "My Neil does the *same* thing!"

Barker narrowed his eyes as he looked down at Jessie, and she did the same to him in only the way she could. Barker held out a hand and cracked a smile.

"*Deal,*" Barker said, slapping his hand into Jessie's. "Sounds reasonable."

"There will be a rent increase, and maybe we can talk some more about the servant stuff, since you brought it up," Jessie said, winking at Julia.

"Don't push your luck!" Barker said as he reached out for his pint. "But maybe while your arm heals."

"Look at you!" Dot exclaimed, clapping her hands together as a grin spread from ear to ear. "You're like a happy family! A strangely cobbled together dysfunctional happy family!"

"I'll take that," Julia said, reaching over Jessie's shoulders to grab Barker's outstretched hand. "I wouldn't change us for the world."

If you enjoyed *Fruit Cake and Fear*, why not sign up to Agatha Frost's **free** newsletter at **AgathaFrost.com** to hear about brand new releases!

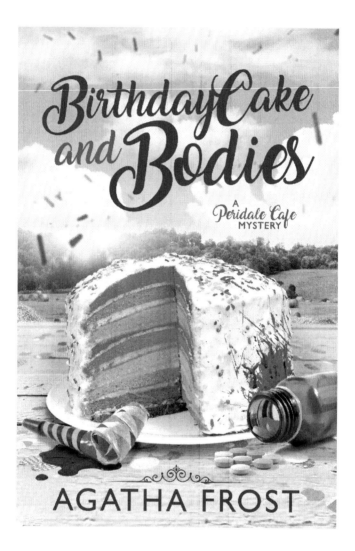

Coming October 17th 2017! Julia and friends
are back for another Peridale Café Mystery case
in *Birthday Cake and Bodies!*

32017842R00148

Printed in Great Britain
by Amazon